Fences

FENCES

A Smith Mountain Lake Novel

Inglath Cooper

Sempre Leggere Press

Contents

Copyright

Can true love ever overcome betrayal?

At eighteen, Tate Callahan left Smith Mountain Lake with no intention of ever coming back. The one thing he'd believed in after a lifetime of growing up in foster homes was his love for Jillie Andrews and her love for him. But a single act of jealousy had destroyed all that, and Tate has spent the past eighteen years trying to convince himself what they had was never real. And he's done a pretty good job of it, until the day someone decides the past isn't better left alone.

When old accusations are brought to light, Tate believes Jillie is responsible and heads back to Smith Mountain Lake to once and for all prove to himself that she is not the woman of his dreams, but the woman who had destroyed his dreams. What he finds though isn't at all what he'd expected. And the question he will have to answer is whether the protective fences we build around ourselves can ever be taken down, letting us see not only what might have been, but what can still be.

"If you like your romance in New Adult flavor, with plenty of ups and downs, oh-my, oh-yes, oh-no, love at first sight, trouble, happiness, difficulty, and follow-your-dreams, look no further than extraordinary prolific author Inglath Cooper. Ms. Cooper understands that the romance genre deserves good writing, great characterization, and true-to-life settings and situations, no matter the setting. I recommend you turn off the phone and ignore the doorbell, as you're not going to want to miss a moment of this saga of the girl who headed for Nashville with only a guitar, a hound, and a Dream in her heart." – **Mallory Heart Reviews**

"Truths and Roses . . . so sweet and adorable, I didn't want to stop reading it. I could have put it down and picked it up again in the morning, but I didn't want to." – **Kirkusreviews.com**

On Truths and Roses: "I adored this book...what romance should be, entwined with real feelings, real life and roses blooming. Hats off to the author, best book I have read in a while." – **Rachel Dove, FrustratedYukkyMommyBlog**

"I am a sucker for sweet love stories! This is definitely one of those! It was a very easy, well written, book. It was easy to follow, detailed, and didn't leave me hanging without answers." – **www.layfieldbaby.blogspot.com**

"I don't give it often, but I am giving it here – the

sacred 10. Why? Inglath Cooper's A GIFT OF GRACE mesmerized me; I consumed it in one sitting. When I turned the last page, it was three in the morning."
– MaryGrace Meloche, Contemporary Romance Writers

5 Blue Ribbon Rating! ". . .More a work of art than a story. . .Tragedies affect entire families as well as close loved ones, and this story portrays that beautifully as well as giving the reader hope that somewhere out there is A GIFT OF GRACE for all of us." — Chrissy Dionne, Romance Junkies 5 Stars

"A warm contemporary family drama, starring likable people coping with tragedy and triumph." 4 1/2 Stars. — Harriet Klausner

"A GIFT OF GRACE is a beautiful, intense, and superbly written novel about grief and letting go, second chances and coming alive again after devastating adversity. Warning!! A GIFT OF GRACE is a three-hanky read...better make that a BIG box of tissues read! Wowsers, I haven't cried so much while reading a book in a long long time...Ms. Cooper's skill makes A GIFT OF GRACE totally believable, totally absorbing...and makes Laney Tucker vibrantly alive. This book will get into your heart and it will NOT let go. A GIFT OF GRACE is simply stunning in every way—brava, Ms. Cooper! Highly, highly recommended!" – 4 1/2 Hearts — Romance Readers Connection

"...A WOMAN WITH SECRETS...a powerful love story laced with treachery, deceit and old wounds that will not heal...enchanting tale...weaved with passion, humor, broken hearts and a commanding love that will have your heart soaring and cheering for a happily-ever-after love. Kate is strong-willed, passionate and suffers a bruised heart. Cole is sexy, stubborn and also suffers a bruised heart...gripping plot. I look forward to reading more of Ms. Cooper's work!" – **www.freshfiction.com**

I never expected anyone to take care of me, but in my wildest dreams and juvenile yearnings, I wanted the house with the picket fence . . .

– Maya Angelou

1

Jillie

"JILLIAN!"

The sound of my name grates in my ears like a razor against glass. I stop at the foot of the winding mahogany staircase, hesitating under a sudden rush of rebellion. I consider not answering.

Eighteen years, and my mother-in-law has never once called me by the name I have always gone by. The first time that Jeffrey brought me home to meet his family, Judith had declared the nickname a quaint, if plebeian, one. Never having heard the word plebian used before, I went home that night and looked it up in the dictionary, my cheeks then burning for days under the slight.

But as quickly as it erupts, the rebellion wilts inside me like a morning glory under noon sun. With resigned steps, I follow the hallway to the library where Judith sits in a leather chair that fans out from behind her shoulders like gargoyle wings. She sips from a porcelain cup of hot tea, her posture Emily Post perfect, her Manolo Blahnik-clad feet neatly crossed at the ankles. The curtains are drawn, blocking out the late afternoon sunlight I am suddenly craving.

Since Jeffrey's death, Judith has kept the house so dark it feels as if we are living in a tomb, choking on the stale air. I want to yank open the curtains, throw the windows wide with their view of Smith Mountain Lake and fill the old house with fresh air and light, let it breathe as it hasn't in far too long.

But as much as I hate it, I am fully aware that if anyone deserves to endure the oppressive gloom here, I do.

Dressed in beige linen pants and a navy silk sweater, a slim gold necklace and matching earrings her only jewelry, Judith looks as if she could have been cut out of a Vogue ad for older customers of haute couture. Her blonde hair hangs in a neat pageboy, and her manicured nails are as perfect now as they had been when she'd left the salon at Westlake three days before.

Appearances are everything in the Taylor household, and I've never once seen my mother-in-law with a single hair out of place. Even after all these years of living under the same roof, I still feel more like an adolescent in her presence than a thirty-six-year-old woman.

"The day certainly sped by, didn't it?" Judith glances at her watch, her voice holding the same pseudo-pleasant note she reserves for bank tellers and post office clerks.

I bite my lip to keep from disagreeing. This day has been like too many others, where I wish away the hours between dropping Kala and Corey off at school in the morning and picking them up again in the afternoon.

"Was there something you wanted me to do while I'm

out?" I ask, assuming there must be some reason I've been summoned.

"Would you mind stopping by the grocery store, Jillian? The Simpsons are coming for dinner tonight, and Lucille said we're a bit short on greens for the salad."

I force a smile to my mouth, an effort that feels like stretching metal.

"I'd be happy to."

"Do be sure to get the arugula and radicchio, won't you? They make such a nice presentation."

"Of course," I say, not missing the subtle reminder of another time years ago when I'd been asked to do the same errand before a dinner party and committed the cardinal sin of arriving home with iceberg lettuce.

Outside the house, I draw in a breath of warm May air, then slide into the black, Mercedes four-wheel drive, putting the vehicle in reverse and rolling down the paved tree-lined driveway that marks the entrance to Stone Meadow. I'll only be gone for an hour or less, and yet leaving the house gives me a sense of release that makes me nearly lightheaded with relief.

I glance in the rearview mirror at the enormous colonial house, grand in every sense of the word. Stone Meadow had been built in 1870, long before Smith Mountain Lake had come to exist. The parts of it that became lakefront property once the lake was completed only increased its value.

Magnolia trees grace the brick sidewalk that leads to the entrance of the house. White columns support the front porch, and pane windows with century-old glass catch the afternoon sunlight.

As one of the premier hunter-jumper farms in Virginia, Stone Meadow once represented everything I dreamed of having in life. The small, white, A-frame house where I'd grown up as the daughter of the farm manager at Cross Country, Stone Meadow's local rival, had been a long way from the Taylor mansion in more ways than one.

And yet, there had been countless nights throughout my marriage to the heir of Stone Meadow when I cried myself to sleep, wishing for the comfort of that little white house. Wishing I could figure out how I'd veered from the path I had been so sure would be mine.

But if I know anything by now, it is that there is no starting over.

Accepting the roads I chose is the only option. Because, after all, I have no one to blame for those choices but myself.

2

Jillie

I PULL UP in front of the Herald Country Day School in Moneta at exactly ten minutes past three, turning in my seat so I can see the girls when they erupt out of the Southern-style structure as they do each afternoon.

Next to seeing their faces first thing in the morning, this is the best part of my day. The bell rings, and the front door opens, children pouring from the building in a giggling kaleidoscope of blue and green school uniforms.

I spot Kala and Corey in the first group, and, as always, my heart tightens at the sight of their smiling faces, their blonde ponytails streaming out behind them.

Fourteen now, Kala is taller than her sister by several inches. She is the serious one, smart and sensitive, rarely without a book in her hand. I worry that she is too serious, more quiet and withdrawn than ever since Jeffrey's death.

Marching along behind her is Corey, at ten, much more carefree than Kala. Every once in a while, she asks if her daddy is in heaven and if he'll come back here to be with them if he doesn't like it there. I struggle to find answers that satisfy my daughter without altering her positive outlook on life. Not an easy thing to do when my own outlook has been so irrevocably changed.

Kala opens the door and climbs in the back. "Hi, honey," I say, smiling the cheerful smile I've managed to perfect for my daughters in the year since Jeffrey's death.

"Hey." Kala's greeting is indifferent and as perfected as my own. She props her knees against the seat in front of her and promptly loses herself in a tattered copy of The Scarlet Letter.

"Are you reading that for school, honey?" I ask.

"No," she answers abruptly. "I just want to."

Corey crawls into the front seat, a cluster of now drooping dandelions clutched in one fist. I lean across to kiss her cheek and smooth a hand across her hair where a stray strand has slipped free of her gold barrette.

No matter how well-brushed it might be when she leaves for school, Corey's hair manages to settle into a mass of tangles by the end of the day. The new white tights I laid out for her that morning now have holes in the knees. She is as much a tomboy as I had been at her age. "How was your day, honey?" I ask.

"Good. I picked these for you at lunchtime," Corey says, holding out the now-wilted flowers. "I gave Miss Crawford some, too. But I saved the best bunch for you."

I take the dandelions, feeling the sincerity of her gesture imprint on my heart. "They're beautiful, honey. Thank you."

I put the car in gear and pull away from the school, guilt for my earlier self-pity stabbing through me. I have no right to that indulgence. On the surface, I have an enviable life. Two beautiful children. A safe and comfortable home in which to raise them.

I often think that if I'd been more appreciative of what I had instead of wishing for something long gone, Jeffrey might have made a different choice in the end. And maybe the nightmare of the past year would never have happened. Maybe I could have found some way to fix what was wrong between us. Maybe my children would still have a father.

3

Jillie

KALA AND COREY want to wait in the car while
I run into the grocery store. They have a riding lesson
at four, so I hurry to pick out the greens, arugula and
radicchio, from the produce department, then head for the
express checkout counter.

A man in front of me with a walker struggles to remove
the items from his basket. I help him place them on the
conveyor belt and then shrug away his surprised gratitude
when he begins to thank me, as if it has been a very long
time since anyone helped him with anything.

While I'm waiting, I glance at the magazines on the
rack beside the checkout. A newly acclaimed actress graces
the cover of *Premiere*, an out-of-control pop star the front
of *People*.

A line of tabloids hangs next to the magazines. The
one in the center snags my attention. I stare for a moment,
and then my arms go suddenly slack, the bags dropping to
the floor. I quickly stoop down and pick them up, aware of

several curious glances being sent my way from shoppers in the neighboring aisles.

Only one copy of the *Revealer* remains on the stand. Hit with a sudden wave of dizziness, I grab it and tuck it beneath my plastic produce bags. Maybe I'm mistaken. Seeing ghosts where there simply aren't any.

I somehow manage to pay the clerk and leave the store, barely aware of pulling the money from my wallet or of crossing the parking lot to the Mercedes until a car sounds its horn, and I realize I've stepped out in front of it. I hurry to the car, open the door, get in, and stuff the grocery bag beneath my seat.

"What's wrong, Mommy?" Corey asks, alarm in her voice. "You're all pale."

Kala scoots up in the backseat, a worried frown creasing her forehead. "Didn't you see that car?" she asks. "It almost hit you."

"I'm sorry, girls," I say, trying for a reassuring smile. "I wasn't paying attention. I didn't mean to scare you. I'm fine. Really."

I start the Mercedes and put it in gear, silently berating my carelessness. Since Jeffrey's death, Corey has been terrified of something happening to me. For the first few months, it had been almost impossible to get her to go to school or anywhere at all without me. Only in the past several weeks has she begun to loosen her hold, to believe that I'm not also going to leave her.

Despite the shell she has encased herself in, I know Kala worries too and that she tries her best to hide it.

And so, struggling for normalcy, I ask each of them about school, what they'd learned in their classes, and whether or not they ate the lunch I packed them that morning. The only sign that anything at all out of the ordinary has happened is my white-knuckled grip on the steering wheel.

4

Tate

FINGERS STILL ON the keyboard, I stare at the screen of my laptop computer.

Two hours so far, and not a word. What's that old saying? Blood from a turnip? That pretty much describes it. Two hours in the chair, and the screen in front of me is still blank.

At the insistence of my agent, Margaret Barnes, I've been holed up for three weeks in an apartment at the Sherry-Netherland, overlooking Central Park. The owner is a friend of Margaret's and since she's spending the spring in Europe, she offered up the place for me to write.

Margaret's proposition had not been a subtle one. "Roving the country in that poor excuse you call a house is no way to get a book written. I don't know how you remember where you are every morning."

This was the part where I had started to interrupt, to tell her that it suited me better not to know. I had refrained though, knowing from past experience that any argument from me would launch her into a dissertation on the lack of reason to be found in the way I prefer to keep my options open. The way I never tie myself to one place for any length of time. Hence, my rolling Airstream home.

"So we'll put you on house arrest until you write the damn book," Margaret had said, handing me the keys to the apartment. "Just write the book, Tate."

Write the book.

The truth is I don't know if I'll ever write another word.

From the Manhattan streets below, comes the sound of honking horns, screeching tires. People alive and living. I drop my head against the back of the chair and stare at the ceiling.

Maybe it's time to give it up. Admit that I'd been a one-book wonder. Exorcised my demons on the page. End of story.

It would make sense.

For a dozen years, I'd made a career out of traipsing the world to cover one horrific news story after the other. I saw things that are impossible to erase from my memory, things unimaginable to the average person living an average life. Children with arms and legs blown away by land mines triggered on the way to get daily water for their family. Women grieving the discovery of a son found among a pile of bodies pushed into a mass grave and barely covered with dirt.

But at some point, the stress migraines that started when I was a kid became a daily occurrence. To the point that getting out of bed was an exercise in torture.

And so, I walked away. Came home to the United States where broken children were not a daily visual, bought a Ford F-350 and an Airstream to pull behind it, and drove the country from one end to the other, trying to immerse myself in the normalcy of small-town diners, where the daily special could always be counted on, and people walked dogs down tree-lined streets. Just normal. And somewhere along the way, a story clamored inside me, insistent enough that I decided to write it just to get it out of my system.

One morning, sitting outside the silver Airstream, staring at a mountain somewhere in Wyoming, I'd turned on my laptop for the first time since returning to the States, started writing, and basically didn't quit until I finished the book six weeks later.

I never intended to show it to anyone, sticking the printed manuscript in a manila folder and labeling that particular chapter from my past closed.

But a few months later, Harley Austin, my former news editor, arranged to meet up with me in Bozeman, Montana. I picked him up at the Bozeman Yellowstone International Airport, immediately spotting him in the procession of people filing off the commuter airplane, his gray hair buzzed to nearly military specifications, his body lean and wiry from the marathons for which he regularly trained. Harley thought I had done the right thing in taking some time off, but the network wanted him to try to get me back.

It took me nearly three days to convince Harley I was done. That I wasn't ever going back. Once he had accepted the failure of his plea mission, he lengthened his stay by a few days, and we spent it fly-fishing in some of Montana's most beautiful rivers.

On the last morning of his visit, I had stepped outside the Airstream to find him holding the folder containing the manuscript I'd spent six weeks writing.

Harley glanced up without a speck of guilt on his face. "Sorry," he said. "I was looking for a notepad in your desk. I told myself I'd only read the first page. I couldn't stop until the very last one. Your fault for writing such a damn compelling story. Any of this true?"

I stared at him too unsettled to answer.

"What are you planning to do with it?" he asked then.

I lifted a shoulder, glanced out at the rolling Montana river, fifty or so yards away. "Decorate my drawer, I guess," I said.

Harley studied me for a moment. "This is good, Tate. Really good. Let me show it to someone. Just see what they say."

He ignored my refusal, and, a week later, I got a call from Margaret.

Harley was a friend of hers, and he'd told her about this amazing book a friend of his had written. She would love to see it.

On a whim, a weak moment, an attack of ego, desire for revenge, or something I'm still not sure of, I sent it to her. Which is exactly how I ended up here in this Manhattan hotel trying to write a second book I can't write.

A knock at the door pulls me from the chair. I open the door to a bellman holding a white envelope. "This just arrived for you at the front desk, sir," he says.

"Thanks." I pull out my wallet and hand him a tip.

The bellman thanks me and disappears down the hotel hallway.

I lay the package on the desk, pour myself another cup of coffee from the silver pot next to the computer, take a sip, and sit back down. I reach for the envelope, tearing open one end and pulling out a tabloid-style newspaper. I unfold it, stare hard at the cover, then drop it on the desk, as if it is a snake in mid-strike.

Numbness seeps up, spreads through my arms and legs like injected poison.

A paper clip holds a note attached to the front page. I pull it loose, recognizing Margaret's handwriting.

Call me after you read this.

A sick feeling knots my stomach.

I don't want to read it. I want to put it back in the envelope, toss it in the trashcan, and pretend I never saw it. But like Pandora's box, impossible.

I pick the paper up again, look at the picture on the cover, the two faces staring back at me failing to resonate, like people I've never met.

A national tabloid known for its lack of standards and we-print-anything approach to publishing, *The Revealer* graces the grocery store racks with headlines like "President Fathers Child With Daughter's Babysitter" and "Aliens Found Living Outside Topeka, Kansas!"

Garbage.

And my name is featured as the banner of this week's edition. "Tate Callahan: Former War Correspondent Turned Bestselling Author Reveals Tarnished Past!"

The photo accompanying it ties a knot in my gut. There is only one person that photo could have come from.

Jillie.

How could she?

That photo was personal, private. From another time in my life. In her life.

Seeing it on the cover of this rag makes a mockery out of every memory I foolishly held onto of her.

I've never seen the picture before now, but I remember

as if it were yesterday, the hot July afternoon at Cross Country Farm when it had been taken. The summer before my senior year in high school. The summer when everything changed between Jillie and me.

She'd brought a camera with her that day and snapped pictures of me for her photo album. She'd then asked one of the guys at the barn to take a picture of us together. Laughing, she'd hopped on my back, her long legs wrapped around my waist, her arms looped around my shoulders, her chin tucked against my neck. The photo caught us both with wide smiles on our faces. A strand of Jillie's long, blonde hair stuck to my cheek.

So long ago.

And yet I remember with complete clarity the feel of her, the softness of her skin against my arms, the smell of her, a hot July breeze tinted with the sweet scent of newly mown hay.

I remember too, going home that afternoon, taking an ice-cold shower and asking myself how much longer I could keep thinking of Jillie Andrews as my best friend. Somehow, when I hadn't been looking, my feelings for her had set out on a course of their own.

Regret, unsummoned, unwelcome, tilts inside me. Unable to stop myself, I pick up the paper and stare at the picture again. I never wanted to love her. Although, somehow, it had never presented itself as optional.

My cell phone rings. I pick it up with an abrupt hello.

"Did you get the paper?" Margaret Barnes has never been one to mince words.

"Thanks for the day brightener." I swing my chair back toward the desk, refusing to look at the tabloid.

"To tell you the truth, it didn't do much for mine, either," she says, a reproachful note in her voice. "As your friend, I wanted to burn the thing. But as your agent, I thought you should see it, so we can talk about damage control."

"Damage control?" My laugh is disbelieving. "You're kidding, right?"

"You're a public figure, Tate," she reasons, as if I'm a child in need of a simple explanation. "People think they have a right to know about you. And I can assure you that your publisher is definitely interested in what you're doing."

I look out the window at the crowded skyline and say, "They published my book, Margaret. They don't own me."

"No. But if you remember correctly, that was a book that's been on bestseller lists for six months running. A book that earned you a noteworthy advance on your current contract. You can't blame them for being just a little nervous about this."

"I didn't do it, Margaret," I say, suddenly weary, hating to even have to say the words.

A too-lengthy stretch of silence follows my assertion. "Do you have any idea who's responsible for this story?"

When I don't answer, she says, "If they've got a personal vendetta against you, this needs to be taken care of quickly and quietly."

"Did you hear the part where I said I didn't do it?"

"I'm not sure that even matters in today's world."

"The hell it doesn't."

"All I'm saying," she says, her voice suddenly soothing, "is that once something is in print, it's difficult to erase."

An old anger stirs inside me. How many years have I tried to outrun the same, tired story only to end up staring it in the face again? "What are you suggesting?"

"Whatever it takes. You have a new future ahead of

you, Tate. I don't want to see it ruined just when it's getting started."

I let out a ragged sigh, the beginnings of a migraine throbbing in my temples. It's been a year since I've had one, and I'd actually begun to think they might have gone away.

How can I expect Margaret to understand what she's asking of me? I went back to Smith Mountain Lake once, and I'd vowed never to do so again. Nothing is worth going back there. Not even the saving of a career I'm not sure I wanted.

Going back means resurrecting a past I only want to forget. I've spent my entire adult life trying to put behind me a childhood that had been less than grand and a teenage dream that ended in a nightmare. And even if I haven't forgiven or forgotten, I can sleep at night.

"Tell me you'll try to fix this, Tate," Margaret says. "Find out who's trying to screw up your life. Please."

I click off the phone without telling her I already know who. The question is why.

5

Jillie

I STOP THE Mercedes in the circular drive of Stone Meadow. While the girls open their doors and scoot out, I pull the magazine from the grocery bag and stuff it in my purse.

Inside the house, I leave the greens on the kitchen counter and then hustle the girls upstairs to change into their riding clothes.

"Aren't you going to watch, Mommy?" Corey asks a few minutes later, as she follows us into the hall and back down the stairs.

"I have some things to do, honey," I say, helping her with the chin strap on her helmet.

"But you always watch us," Kala says, suspicion in her voice.

"I'll come down before you finish."

"You're not going anywhere, are you?" Corey asks, her dark eyes clouded with worry.

"Of course not. I'll even peek at you out of the window of my room."

"Okay," Corey says.

Kala heads for the barn without saying anything else, an I-don't-care-anyway set to her shoulders.

I watch them for a moment, feeling my oldest daughter's distance. I go back upstairs then, close my bedroom door and lock it. Leaning against the frame, I stare at the enormous bedroom I long ago grew to dislike.

It's the same one I shared with Jeffrey, the furniture dark and heavy, the curtains a dense burgundy that makes me think of the bottle of port found next to his dead body. I wonder, as I have many times, if he'd needed the liquid courage to do what he'd done. And then I feel instantly guilty for the thought. When did I become so unkind?

I pull my purse from the walnut dresser drawer and dump the contents onto the bed. Snatching the tabloid out of the rubble, I sink into the chair by the window. Turning it over, a profusion of emotions again assaults me.

From the cover, Tate Callahan's smiling face looks back at me. His young, good-looking face, exactly as I remember it. Exactly as it looked on the pages of the photo album where I'd kept this same picture since the day I took it so many years ago.

For a moment, I let myself dwell on the memory of hair, dark as molasses, and thick-lashed eyes that had a way of reading my thoughts before I could ever voice them.

Tate.

He'd made something out of his life. Just as I had always known he would. I've kept up with him through the papers, saved the articles written about him in various magazines, tucking them away in a trunk inside my closet. It has been a long, long time since I let myself take them out and think about the years when he had been my best friend, when for a brief time, he had been so much more.

Inside the walk-in closet sits a trunk, on top of which I keep my winter sweaters. I sweep them to the floor and open the lid. Here, I keep all my important documents and other personal things. The girls' birth certificates. My mother's wedding band. The album in which I had put away all visual reminders of Tate.

I haven't looked at it in years, and yet I know exactly where the picture should be. I flip to the page, only to find a blank spot in its place. My heart drops.

I look down at the tabloid again, aware suddenly that the girl in the photo no longer exists. At the upper, right hand corner of the page is a current picture of Tate, a somber photo of a handsome man I had once planned on spending my life with.

I can see that he has changed, matured, his features somehow leaner, his blue eyes registering disillusion and life lived. I skim the text beneath the article, my stomach dropping a little more with each line.

Bestselling author Tate Callahan is pictured above with childhood sweetheart Jillie Andrews of Smith Mountain Lake, Virginia. Sources tell us the two broke up when then eighteen-year-old Callahan was charged with the attempted rape of a sixteen-year-old girl. Readers may be interested to learn the probable source of the angst that propelled his first novel to the top of bookstore bestseller lists after it was chosen as Book of the Month by national talk show . . .

I drop the paper, as if it has suddenly burned me.

Someone has been digging into Tate's past, and I have no doubt that he will believe me responsible for this.

But then in the past twenty years, nothing has brought Tate back to Smith Mountain Lake. A picture on the cover of a cheap tabloid is hardly likely to do so.

In the back of the trunk, the corner of a high school annual catches my eye. A faded envelope sticks out of the top. I start to reach for it, then quickly slam the trunk lid shut. I should have thrown it away long ago.

That and every other sentimental reminder of him. How many times had Jeffrey asked what I kept hidden in this trunk, silently imploring me to get rid of the past once and for all?

I'd never been able to do so. And maybe, in the big picture, that says it all.

6

Jillie

I HAVE TO GET out. Go for a drive. Just long enough to clear my head.

An evening with Judith and her guests has stretched me so tight that I feel like a rubber band about to snap. Even when Jeffrey had been alive, I never felt comfortable at those dinners, always aware of Judith's subtle reminders that I didn't belong in the Taylor household.

I check on the girls, who are both asleep, and then grab my purse and keys, silently taking the steps to the front door. Leaving the lights off, I let the Mercedes roll down the driveway until I'm out of sight of the house. Near the bottom, I flick them on and pull onto the main road.

Stars shine in the sky overhead, a quarter moon suspended in its own corner. I press the accelerator hard, the needle on the speedometer inching higher, higher. Sixty-five. Seventy.

The speed feels good. In fact, it feels great.

For a few moments, I let myself believe I can outrun all

the things that are wrong in my life, in the same way I had once believed I could ride my horse to a life far different from the one I'd been born to.

And just for a moment, I want to be truly selfish. It would be easy, really. A slip of the tire to the edge of the pavement. A tree on the side of the road. It would take no more than that. And all my regrets would be gone.

Every single one of them.

The speedometer inches forward, topping eighty-five. Did Jeffrey have these same thoughts? Did the same war wage inside him?

But then I see the sweet faces of my two daughters, as I had left them sleeping. Guilt slices through me. I put my foot on the brake, slow the car to the speed limit. The needle has just leveled off at fifty-five when headlights suddenly flash in the rearview mirror.

The car comes out of nowhere, racing up behind me, its front end almost touching the Mercedes' bumper. I touch the brake again, and the car falls back a short distance, then shoots around me in a black flash, even though the double yellow lines indicate a no-passing zone.

Thirty yards ahead, the car slams to a stop in the middle of the road and swings around at a ninety-degree turn, tires squalling.

I fumble for the door lock, fear a sudden, choking knot in my chest.

I'm in the middle of nowhere, not a house in sight. A black Porsche 911 with New York plates now blocks both lanes in front of me. It's hardly the kind of car someone who needs to steal a vehicle would be driving.

I grip the wheel until my knuckles lose their color. I'll go around it. The shoulder is steep, but it beats waiting to see what this lunatic has in mind. A few moments ago,

I'd foolishly wondered what it would be like to leave it all behind. Now, adrenaline fuels an undeniable rush of survival instinct.

I stomp on the accelerator, but just then the car door opens, and a man climbs out. The headlights catch his profile. I slam on the brakes again, feeling the blood leave my face.

The front bumper of the Mercedes stops just short of his knees. I sit, frozen to the seat, my hands glued to the steering wheel.

Disbelief weighs like a rock on my chest.

How many times have I wondered what it would be like to see him again? Imagined what I would say to him?

In what feels like slow motion, I unlock the door and get out, barely aware of my feet touching the ground.

"Are you trying to kill yourself?" he asks, walking toward me.

The voice is a surprise. Deep and even, it is the voice of a man, not the boy I remember.

"Apparently so," he says, when I don't answer. He slides inside my car and pulls it over to the shoulder of the road. He gets back out again, my keys in his hand.

His highhandedness strikes a nerve. "Give me back my keys," I say.

Again, he ignores me, tossing them up and catching them in his palm, before turning and making his way back to his own car.

I stand there for a moment, feeling as if some ridiculous gauntlet has been thrown.

The taillights from the car cast him in silhouette. He is as tall as I remember, but his shoulders are wider than they had once been. His slightly wavy hair touches the collar of his light-blue shirt. He opens the car door and slides inside. "Get in, Jillie," he says without looking at me.

"We need to talk."

"There's nothing for us to talk about," I say.

"That the best you can do after all these years?"

We stare at each other for what feels like a long time, neither of us willing to back down.

Finally, I take a deep breath and count to five before going around to the passenger side and opening the door.

I'll stay long enough to get my keys back and let him have his say.

No sooner have I gotten in than he reaches across me and pulls the door closed. He slaps the lock button behind the gear shift, securing the doors with a solid-sounding wachunk. He snaps my seat belt into place.

"Tate, stop," I say in the most reasonable voice I can manage. "This is crazy. Let me out of the car."

But he turns the key and shoves the gearshift into first, slamming the accelerator to the floor. The car shoots down the narrow road with a deafening roar.

He pushes another button, and the top slides back. The star-clustered sky hangs above us like a beaded canopy.

The wind catches my hair, the car taking the curves effortlessly, hugging the road like a fine leather glove on a woman's hand. I glance at the speedometer. The needle hits ninety, inching higher.

I grip the door handle. Ninety-five. One hundred.

We are flying now, the trees a blur by the side of the road, the yellow line dividing the pavement in front of us nearly invisible. I say nothing, feeling his gaze on me, but staring straight ahead and refusing to look at him.

Another minute or two passes before he stands on the

brake and swings the car onto a dirt road barely visible amidst the overbrush on each side of it.

I remember this road.

It leads to a dead end where it meets the lake. Tate had taken me parking here one night during our senior year in high school. I haven't been here since, but the same pasture stretches out to our right, moonlight glancing off the grass. Several large black and white cows turn to let out questioning moos.

Tate cuts the engine and the headlights at the same time. "Nerves of steel. You always had them, didn't you, Jillie?" he asks softly, a grudging note of respect in his voice. "There was never a jump too high for you."

"You don't scare me, Tate. As much as you might want to."

"And me an attempted rapist." The words were quietly issued, but there was no mistaking their razor edge.

"I know you didn't do it," I say, the words barely audible.

He laughs, a bitter laugh I don't recognize at all.

I remember other times when we had laughed together, over silly things, like using a fallen tree as a balance beam and ending up in the creek together, both of us going in head first only to emerge with our clothes stuck to us in places that had us staring first in healthy curiosity and then in lustful longing.

"What makes you so sure now?" he asks, his voice at once belligerent and yet hoarse around the edges.

"I know you would never have done that."

"You didn't know that then. You see, Jillie, I have a good memory. And I remember the look in your eyes the day you came to see me in jail. You believed it."

Pain, long thought resolved, stabs through me. "Tate—"

"How much did they pay you for the photo?" he asks in a voice casual enough to be inquiring about the weather.

"If you're talking about the magazine that just came out, I had nothing to do with it."

"Was it for the money?" he goes on, as if I haven't denied it. "I should think you have plenty of that now."

"The picture was in my—" I stop there, start again. Too much information. "I didn't send it to them."

"Then who did?"

I realize that it won't matter what I say. He won't believe me. "I don't know."

He stares at me for several long seconds before getting out of the car.

I wait a minute or two, then open my door. I walk to the front where he is leaning against the hood. The night air is cool on my arms. "If this is causing problems with your career, I'm sorry, but—"

His gaze locks with mine. "My career. You think that's all this is about?"

The question sends an arrow straight through me. All these years since we've seen each other, and I still know him. With other people, he always managed a good front to his feelings. But from day one, it had never worked with me. Shocking to realize it still doesn't. "I don't know what to say."

His gaze holds mine for several long seconds. "I've been asked to make sure you don't have any more cards up your sleeve. So here goes. Do you?"

Bitterness saturates the words. He means for them to hurt. And they do.

"I told you. I had nothing to do with it."

"So who did?"

"I don't know."

"Not exactly the answer I'm looking for." He shoves away from the car then, swinging around to stand in front of me.

A warning bell goes off inside me. Close. Too close.

For long, drawn-out seconds, he says nothing. He just stands there, looking down at me. His gaze lingers on my face, then drops lower in deliberate appraisal. I force myself not to move, when all innate survival instinct demands I run.

I lift my chin an inch or two higher and stand my ground.

He looks his fill, then meets my gaze, and says, "Jillie Andrews. All grown up."

It isn't a compliment. I don't take it as one. Instead, I return the perusal, my gaze dropping from his face to his chest, subtly defined beneath the blue shirt. I glance away, unable to continue holding up my flagging confidence.

"Or maybe not so grown up, after all," he says.

I push away from the car, forcing him to move. "Take me back. I can assure you there won't be any more photos of the two of us floating around," I say, emphasizing the last. "As soon as I get home, I'm going to burn every last one of them."

He catches my arm, studying my face. "So why didn't you before?"

The directness of his gaze robs me of a response. "I realize now I should have," I finally manage.

"You sent them that picture." A statement, not a question.

"Believe what you want, Tate," I say, stepping away and heading for the car door.

But he reaches for me again, this time pinning me to the hood in a lightning-quick movement, his legs pressing into mine. With one hand, he holds my wrists above my head. "Isn't this what you would expect of me, Jillie? Rough and tumble? Is this what you imagined me doing with Angela? Not as nice and innocent as what we did?"

I keep my gaze locked with his, refusing to look away, as if in doing so, I might lose something I'd never be able to get back again.

"Well, is it?" he asks when I don't answer, his voice noticeably hoarser than before. "Are you afraid of me? Afraid the way Angela said she was of that barbaric Callahan boy?"

Given the look on his face, maybe I'm a fool, but of all the emotions descending over me, fear is not one of them.

The hood of the car is cool beneath my shirt, its unforgiving surface making me all the more aware of the muscled lines of the man above me. Memories of a warm spring afternoon when I had all but thrown myself at him come taunting.

Somewhere behind us, an owl hoots, and a breeze lifts the limbs of the white pines to the side of the car. I look into the blue of his eyes and catch a glimpse of the boy I had once known. Uncertainty flickers there. Along with a hint of something else I once thought I'd seen in his eyes when he looked at me.

His gaze drops to my lips. Seconds tick by while we remain still, suspended in indecision. My mouth goes suddenly dry. Tate releases my wrists, and I can see the battle of emotion playing across his face.

He wants to kiss me. I know it without question. I also know how much he hates himself for it.

And yet I want him to.

He lowers his head then, blocking out the Moon behind us. His mouth takes mine, sudden, forceful. Any initial resistance slides away, and I don't want to think. For now, I just want to forget about the awful guilt eating a hole inside me and the mess I've made of my life.

And somewhere near the base of my soul, I want to see if his kiss is as sweet as I remember it.

It is.

And then some.

His mouth all but devours mine, filling me up and draining me at once. With a single kiss, he has already reached more of me than I ever allowed my own husband to reach throughout the duration of our marriage.

With Jeffrey, I'd always held a piece of myself in reserve. A part of me that he could never touch. Maybe I hadn't realized that until now. It seems hateful and beneath me. And I feel ashamed of the kind of wife I'd ended up being.

The realization douses me with the cold shock of ice water.

What am I doing? Tate and I are no longer two teenagers controlled by impulse. We are grown adults with a history, a painful one at that.

I push him away, then slide off the hood and put a few feet of distance between us, my breathing coming in short, ragged gasps.

He stares at me, like someone awakened from a daze, wiping the back of his hand across his mouth, as if he could just as easily wipe away any trace of me. He backs up until a larger chunk of space separates us.

"Why don't you take that home to Jeffrey? I'm sure he'll be waiting to finish what I started."

I flinch, the cool air suddenly chilling my heated skin.

He doesn't know. Stunned, I start to tell him, but something stops me. I don't want to see pity on his face. The last thing in the world I want from Tate Callahan is pity.

7

Tate

I LET THE CAR ROLL to a stop beside the Mercedes, keeping my gaze trained straight ahead, silent.

Without a word, Jillie gets out and slides into her own vehicle before driving away, taillights disappearing into the night. Going back to her husband with my kiss still warm on her mouth.

I slam my palm against the steering wheel, muttering a few choice words when pain explodes through my wrist.

I shove the gearshift into first and swing the car around in the road, heading back toward town. I leave the top down, the wind narrowing my eyes, the painful sting welcome.

What the hell was I thinking to come here, anyway? Leaving New York this morning like a madman on a mission and driving straight through to Virginia had been a crazy, stupid thing to do.

Okay, so I can admit that now. I'll be out of here with the light of day. If Jillie wants to sell the tabloids more stories, it's fine by me. She can tell them whatever she wants to tell them. I'm not going to hang around long enough to dredge up a past I only want to forget.

In the Beginning

WE WERE UNLIKELY friends, she a born optimist, me beaten down by a childhood that unfolded from one foster home chapter to another.

Jillie was sure the world was on the right track, and, like the return of spring after winter, everything always worked out as it was supposed to.

I had lived a decidedly different experience. When we'd first started hanging around together, she felt sorry for me. I knew it. Not because I was the new kid in school, but because as far as she was concerned, it was an awful thing to see the world in shades of gray.

But by the age of seven, I had mastered the art of moving. To me, another school was just another school. There would be the requisite bully, the class princess, and the girl who felt sorry for the new guy and wanted to make it all better.

The bully was Todd Bendermeier, responsible for the most recent bruise beneath my eye. The princess was Angela Taylor, heir apparent to the textile factory where half the town worked and whose honor Todd had apparently been defending. The girl was Jillie Andrews, now hovering around me like a bee to a spring flower, aiming a wet brown paper towel at my throbbing eye.

"I tried to get some ice from the cafeteria," she said, "but the door was locked. This might help."

I took the towel, not because I wanted it, but because she looked so intent on helping that I didn't have the heart to ask her to leave me alone, which was all I really wanted. That and to save enough money to finally strike out on my own. Find some place where I might actually be wanted and never leave. "Thanks," I said, not looking at her.

We sat at the edge of the playground, backs against a set of monkey bars.

"Todd's just jealous," she said. "And he looks worse than you do, if that makes you feel better."

I made a sound of disbelief.

"Well, he does. Everybody knows he's been after her since first grade."

"He won't get any arguments from me."

"Yeah, but Angela gets all googly-eyed every time she looks at you."

"Googly-eyed?"

"You know. Weak at the knees. Heart palpitations."

I choked back a laugh and couldn't stop myself from looking at her. Really looking at her. She had a nice smile: straight, white teeth, lips that looked like she'd just eaten a bowl full of strawberries. Blue eyes with dark lashes made a noticeable contrast to her light-blonde hair. She wore a white, sleeveless blouse with faded jeans and a pair of worn brown boots.

"Why are you so interested in it?"

She lifted a shoulder, traced a finger through the red clay dirt between them.

"Boredom, I guess."

The answer surprised me. She was supposed to say she felt sorry for him. Or it wasn't fair that the new guy always got picked on. A future warrior for the underprivileged. "Glad I could liven up your day," I said.

"Me, too." She smiled again, and I wondered if my take on Jillie Andrews was all wrong. At first glance, she was more plain than pretty; her hair pulled back in a ponytail, her nose dotted with freckles. Unlike Angela whose shiny, dark hair hung to her waist. Angela, who looked as if she'd never been allowed to play in the sun without a hat on. "So how long are you here for?" Jillie asked.

I shot her another look of surprise. "What makes you think it's not forever?"

"Because you look like somebody who can't wait to be sprung."

"No longer than I have to be," I admitted.

She considered my answer. "Where do fourteen year olds go when they're making their own choices?"

Tate pressed a finger against his eye. "Anywhere other than here."

"It's not so bad," she said, sounding offended.

"Been here all your life?" I asked.

"Yep," she said, obviously proud of the fact.

"That's a good thing?"

"What's wrong with roots?"

"I guess nothing, if they're in the right place."

"To me, this is the right place." She waved a hand at the Virginia mountains in the distance, the late September trees starting to turn a series of molten golds and reds.

It was pretty. I could give her that.

I'd spent the early years of my childhood in a forest of concrete, government-built skyscrapers with playgrounds that measured in square feet, rusted sliding boards and rotting seesaws. When I came to live with my current foster family, my first glimpse of the Blue Ridge Mountains made me think the whole thing had to be some kind of cruel joke. That I couldn't actually live in a place this beautiful, that with a single blink it would all disappear, as anything good always had.

Hearing Jillie's unquestioning certainty, I couldn't find a sarcastic response that didn't make me sound like a complete jerk. "If it's so great, what do you do for fun around here?" I asked.

"Ride horses. Hang out at the lake. What else?"

Despite my attempt at indifference, I was intrigued. "You have your own horse?"

White teeth pulled at her bottom lip. "No, but someday I will."

"So whose do you ride?"

"The Mason's. My dad manages their farm. It's—"

"Cross Country. Yeah, I've seen it. Some place."

"Come out some time, and we'll go for a ride. They won't mind."

I shrugged, as if the invitation was no big deal. I'd been in a half dozen different foster homes since the age of seven. Had long ago chosen the route of loner. It was easier. That way you didn't miss anybody too much when you were gone.

Jillie got up, scuffed the toe of her paddock boot in the dirt and shoved her hands in the pockets of her jeans. "If you change your mind, come on by. I'll be riding on Saturday."

I nodded again. No big deal.

"Well. I'll see ya, Tate Callahan," she said.

"See ya, Jillie Andrews."

I watched her walk away, wishing with a sudden fierceness I couldn't explain that she would turn around and come back. But she kept walking, shoulders hunched forward a little under the sting of rejection.

I glanced out at the mountains in the distance. So maybe they weren't going anywhere, anytime soon.

Jillie was halfway across the playground when I jumped to my feet and ran after her. "Hey! Jillie, wait!"

She turned then and smiled, as if she had known I was coming all along.

8

Jillie

I LET MYSELF in the front door of the house without turning on the lights.

"Midnight rendezvous?"

Angela steps into the strip of light shining through the window from the outside porch. Still dressed from the day in a gray suit, she says, "Corey woke up calling for you. Mother was upset when we couldn't find you."

"Is she all right?" I ask quickly.

"I stayed with her until she fell asleep," she says, not bothering to hide her criticism. No one blames me for Jeffrey's death as much as his sister Angela, and she welcomes any opportunity to point out my shortcomings where my daughters are concerned.

Refusing to let it get to me, I run up the stairs, part of me wanting to tear into her about the photo that had mysteriously gone missing from my album. But I don't because I need time to get my thoughts together first.

At the door to the girls' room, I slowly turn the knob

and go inside, tiptoeing across the wood floor. They are both asleep. Since Jeffrey's death, Corey refuses to sleep in her own room, and will only go to sleep curled up next to Kala.

Moonlight shines through the part in the rose-print curtains covering the window, casting shadows across their angelic faces. Regret gnaws at me for having left them tonight.

It's been a while since Corey woke crying, and I hadn't planned to be gone so long. But then I'd never imagined the night turning out as it had. Still, I feel incredibly guilty.

I sit on the side of the bed, smoothing a hand across Corey's silky hair.

She stirs, her eyes opening slightly.

"Mommy?"

"Shh," I whisper. "It's okay, honey. I'm right here."

"We couldn't find you," she says, her voice trembling. "I thought you left. Like Daddy did."

"Oh, baby, I'm not going to leave you," I say, my voice cracking in half.

"I just went out for a little while. You go back to sleep. I'll stay right here with you until you do."

"Promise?" she asks, her eyelids heavy.

"Yes, sweetie. I promise." I tuck the cover around her and kiss her forehead. I reach for her hand and clutch it between mine.

I sit with her until she drifts off again. Once I'm sure they are both sleeping soundly, I go to my own room, closing the door on a heavy sigh.

It's almost three in the morning. I feel exhausted, and at the same time, wide awake.

I run a hot bath, shrug out of my clothes and sink into

the sudsy warmth of the water. I think of the look on Angela's face at the foot of the stairs.

Had she sent the picture to that tabloid? If so, why? What could she possibly stand to gain?

I think of Tate then, still feel his touch on my skin.

So many years. And yet when he had looked at me tonight with his see-everything eyes, all that time dissolved into nothingness. Just nothing.

As if I've been holding my breath until the day he returned, and now I can finally breathe again.

Crazy.

But then it had always been that way with Tate.

My feelings for him weren't something over which I'd ever had any say. I had never been able to turn them off at will. And they led me to do things I came to regret.

More than once.

A few minutes later, I climb out of the tub, drying off with quick, frustrated swipes. In the bedroom, I stare at the closet door before crossing the rug-covered floor to open it.

Inside, I drop onto my knees and pull the key from beneath the trunk where I left it earlier that afternoon. I unlock it and open the lid, pulling out the yellowed envelope I'd refused to look at before.

My name is scrawled across the front in Tate's familiar handwriting. I smooth my thumb across the letters, then turn the envelope over and pull out the crinkled paper. I unfold it, my gaze following the words, even though they are long committed to memory, each and every one.

Dear Jillie,
I thought you were the one person who saw me as I am, who

really knew me. I realize now how wrong I was about that. I think we both know things can never be the same between us.

Tate

I refold the last letter I ever received from him, rubbing my thumb across its time-worn surface and swallowing back the knot of emotion in my throat. Amazing that it had all ended with that. Just that. Even now, the words have no less power over me than they'd had the first time I read them.

For a long time, I told myself that he would change his mind, that he would come back. It wasn't possible that he could leave and I would never see him again.

But I had been wrong. So very, very wrong.

When It Could Have Been Forever

I MADE IT MY goal to make Tate see the lake and our county as a place he didn't ever want to leave.

My reasons were entirely selfish. I wanted him to stay. So I took him to all my favorite places, showed him my favorite things. The top of Smith Mountain where you could see for what looked like miles when the leaves were off the trees. The best cove for swimming. Carl's Place off Route 40, where the homemade coconut pie was the best around. And Smith Mountain Dock, where the carp got fed year-round and greeted customers like old friends.

And eventually, they became his favorite things, too.

But the best thing by far that I had to share with him was Cross Country Farm.

My dad was the manager, and it was owned by Dr. Mason, a cardiologist with a practice in Washington, D.C. The horses were his wife's hobby, but she'd turned it into a business. She had an eye for a talented horse, and many of the yearlings from Cross Country went on to become world-class jumpers.

I lived with my dad in the small, white house close to the big barn. I grew up helping him clean stalls, put out hay, or exercise the horses for Mrs. Mason. Whatever it took to be around them.

It was on a September afternoon that Tate rode the school bus home with me, intent on asking Mrs. Mason for a part-time job. We got off at the top of the long driveway, backpacks anchored on our shoulders, each of us carrying a half-eaten candy bar.

The house sat a quarter mile or so ahead, two enormous old oaks in the front yard, the big, white barn just to the right of it. The far end of one of the pastures sloped down to the lake's edge. A fishing boat buzzed in the distance. I had seen the view too many times to count, but I never grew tired of it.

"I could spend the rest of my life here," I said, looking out at the horses grazing behind the white-board fenced pasture.

"But you don't own it," Tate said.

"No. I never will, but I'm still lucky to live here."

"Don't you want something of your own?" he asked.

I shrugged. "I guess I don't see it that way. Dr. and Mrs. Mason have been good to me and my dad."

Tate kicked at some loose gravel on the asphalt drive. "Maybe I should come back another day."

I whacked him on the shoulder. "No chickening out!"

"They probably don't need any more help," he said, making a less-than-convincing display of indifference.

"If I didn't think they needed the help, I would never have suggested it."

And that was true. What I didn't add was that having Tate work here at Cross Country would be that much more time I got to spend with him.

And next to riding, being with him was my favorite thing. During the past year, we'd become best friends. He came out to the farm on weekends. I taught him how to ride on Goldie, a Hanoverian school horse as kind and gentle as she was pretty.

Before Tate, I'd never really had a best friend. I'd had friends, but no one who liked to do the same things I liked to do. No one who liked books the way I liked them or didn't think it was dumb to talk about them.

For me, Tate was like finding lost treasure, or some other unexpected discovery whose worth had no measure. He was smart and funny, not to mention all the girls acted ridiculous around him.

Especially Angela Taylor. Angela, who was used to the world being served up to her on a silver platter. And in whom Tate wasn't the least bit interested.

I went to church with my dad every Sunday morning, so I'd learned long ago that it wasn't right to take pleasure in someone else's misfortune.

But wrong as it might have been, I wanted Tate for myself. Even if it was amazing that he would want to hang around me, when Angela had all but put out billboards announcing her feelings for him.

Tate stopped in the driveway now, his eyes clouded with uncertainty.

"I'll come back another time," he said.

I put a hand on my hip, gave him a level look. "So what's this really about?"

"I think I might need to practice some more before—"

"You ride nearly as well as I do, and I've been riding my

whole life!" I grabbed his hand and pulled him down the road. "Come on. Once it's over, you'll be glad I made you."

My dad met us outside the big barn doors. In one hand, he held a pitchfork, a wide smile on his face. Tall with long legs and skin browned by years in the sun, he had a way of instantly putting others at ease. I'd always been proud of that about him.

Whenever Tate was there, he followed my father around like a puppy, asking question after question. Tate liked to know the how and why of everything, and so did my dad. Sometimes, I wondered if Tate came to the farm to see him as much as he did to see me.

"Hey, kids," my dad said. "How was school?"

"Good," I said. "Is Mrs. Mason around?"

"She's in the ring out back riding that hellion she calls Sweet Pea."

"Great! Come on, Tate." I grabbed his arm again, guiding him around to the other side of the barn.

"So where's the fire?" my dad called out after us.

"Tate's going to ask her for a job!"

"About time he started doing some work around here," he said with a chuckle.

Sonya Mason was one of those women who looked like she'd been born to ride.

Nearly as tall as my father and skinny as a fence post, she could eventually convince even the most uncooperative of horses to come around to her way of thinking. Sweet Pea ranked high on the uncooperative list. She liked to change her mind about taking a jump the moment you thought she was all set to sail over it.

Tate and I stopped at the ring fence. We planted our arms on the top board, quietly watching. Mrs. Mason cantered the young horse once around, then directed her to the jump. The mare's muscles stiffened in refusal. Mrs. Mason reached down, rubbed her neck as if to say it was okay, and over they went. I began clapping wildly.

Mrs. Mason stopped the mare at the other end of the ring, reached in her pocket and leaned over.

"What's she giving her?" Tate asked.

"A peppermint. It's her reward."

He grinned. "So she'll jump for candy?"

"Everybody has their weakness, I guess."

Mrs. Mason trotted the mare over, coming to a stop at the rail. "So what'd you think?" she asked, directing a smile at the two of us.

"That's the highest I've seen her jump," I said.

"Best yet. For a second there, I thought we weren't going."

"What if you run out of peppermints?" Tate asked.

Mrs. Mason laughed. "I guess we won't be jumping that day."

I elbowed Tate. "Mrs. Mason. Tate has something to ask you."

She unbuckled the chin strap of her helmet, pulled it off, and let it rest on one thigh. "What is it, Tate?"

He dropped a glance at the ground, then looked her in the eye. "I wondered if you needed some extra help around here."

My heart started pounding hard. I'd been nearly certain Mrs. Mason would say yes, but what if she didn't? I crossed my fingers and said a silent please, please, please!

Mrs. Mason studied him for a long moment, and then said, "We can always use another pair of hands. That is, if you're willing to do whatever needs to be done."

"Yes, ma'am," Tate said, a kind of quiet pleasure on his face.

"After school and on weekends?"

"Yes, ma'am," he said again.

"As long as you don't let it interfere with your schoolwork, you can start today."

A huge grin broke across Tate's face. "Thank you, Mrs. Mason."

"Why don't you help Jillie get her horses worked this afternoon? Then maybe on Monday, I'll add a couple more to the list."

"Thank you, Mrs. Mason," we said in unison.

"Better get busy," she said.

For the next two hours, we rode in the ring, giving each horse the workout Mrs. Mason had taught me, from warm-up to cool down.

On the last two horses, I called out to Tate, who'd just cleared a jump on the other end of the ring. "Let's hack out for the cool down."

He waved a hand in agreement, then trotted to the open gate.

The sun was sinking fast, but the air was still warm. A dirt road led along one of the fenced pastures. We walked the big Warmbloods on a long rein.

"So what'd you think?" I asked.

"I can't believe I'm actually going to get paid for this," he said.

"I know. Sometimes I feel like I should be paying her."

We walked on a bit, silent.

"Why didn't the Masons ever have children?" he asked after a while.

"I think they tried, but couldn't."

"Why is it that people who want them can't have them and people who don't end up with half a dozen?"

I heard the disgust in his voice, knew it came from

some painful place inside him. "I guess it's not always like that."

He gave me a look that said he knew infinitely more about the subject than I did.

I'd never asked him about his parents. It always felt as if he kept a wall around the subject, but I wondered now if he might need to talk about it. "What happened to your mom and dad?"

He was quiet for a long time, and then, "When I was six, they went out partying one night and never came back."

"I'm sorry," I said, touching a hand to his shoulder.

"Yeah, me, too."

A knife of empathy sliced through my chest. From the first day I met Tate, I somehow knew he didn't easily let people in. For whatever reason, he had let me in, and I never wanted to give him reason to regret it.

A creek lay at the bottom of the next hill. We stopped there, got off, let the horses have a drink.

"My mom left when I was little," I said softly, surprising myself with the admission.

He looked at me, surprised. "I'm sorry."

"Don't be. I'm not. The way I see it, I'd rather her be gone if this wasn't where she wanted to be. My dad still hurts over it, though. I'd change that if I could."

"Some hurts never go away, I guess," he said.

"I guess not." I reached out then and took his hand. We stood there for a while, the fading sun throwing shadows through the trees by the creek.

And I knew a sudden grounding sense of happiness. Felt as though the holes inside both of us might have lost some of their depth for the simple fact that we had found each other.

9

Angela

IN THE OFFICE off the main living room, Angela sits in front of the flat computer screen, staring at the list of e-mails she has no desire to open.

Work and more work. That was what Jeffrey had left her. A legacy she had not asked for. Did not want. But it is what her mother expects, and so she's taken over where her brother left off.

What her mother expects.

If her life has a through line, this is it. Mother's expectations. No getting around them. They surround her like fencing in a maximum- security prison.

"What are you doing up?"

She starts at the sound of her mother's voice, feeling instantly guilty for her thoughts. Sometimes, Angela believes her mother deliberately sneaks up on her. Sometimes, she wonders if she can read her thoughts.

Angela clicks on one of the e-mails, lifting her

shoulders in a casual shrug. "Just getting a head start on tomorrow."

Judith sits down in the leather chair angled at one end of the desk. "Where did Jillian go this evening?"

Angela looks up in surprise. "I have no idea."

"I heard you talking in the foyer. Did you ask her?"

"Do you think she would have told me if I had?" She aims her voice at neutral, but fails to keep the edge from it.

"I won't have her making a spectacle of this family," Judith says. "Jeffrey has been gone no more than a—"

"Year, Mother. He's been gone a year. Of his own choosing, I might add."

Judith shoots up from the chair, tightening the belt to her white robe with two precise motions. "I will not tolerate that kind of belligerence from you, young lady. You would do well to remember it." She leaves the room then, a cloud of wounded disapproval in her wake.

Angela stares after her mother, flinching at the quiet click of the office door, the sound more effective than a slam.

A wave of resentment rolls over her. She banks it down with well-practiced resolve. It does no good to buck the system. One goes along to get along.

She puts her hand on the computer mouse, clicks on old mail. Opens the letter she'd received at work earlier that day.

Old memories fade, but never really go away, do they?

The words send a chill through her now, just as they had the first time she'd read them.

She backs out of her e-mail, clicking over to documents, where she'd stored the attached file that came with the message.

The photo shows a younger version of her sister-in-law

with Tate Callahan. Both smiling back at her. A moment of happiness forever frozen in a single snapshot.

The email address isn't one she knows. Who would have sent this to her? And why?

Angela stares at the picture. How many times as a young girl had she wished for Tate to look at her that way? Wondered what Jillie had that she didn't.

She tries to dredge up the old hatred, wrap herself in it so the memories don't hurt so much. But the hatred doesn't come. The only emotion she can summon is regret.

Twenty-Two Years Ago

JEALOUSY WAS ABOUT to eat a hole inside her.

Angela stood beside the Stone Meadow Farm horse trailer, tidying the braids of her horse's mane, her fingers quick and nimble at the task.

The Cross Country Farm Classic was held every fall on the first Saturday in October at Smith Mountain Lake. Angela had been entering the show since she was six and had consistently won blue ribbons every year.

This year, at sixteen, her only competition, as far as she could tell, was Jillie Andrews and the big, chestnut mare that belonged to Sonya Mason.

But it wasn't being entered in the same classes with Jillie and the enviable mare that had Angela green with jealousy.

She glanced at the white barn across the stretch of grass where the trailers were parked.

Just outside the sliding front doors, Jillie stood dressed in show breeches and a navy blazer. Beside her, Tate Callahan held the reins of the mare. Jillie was talking about something, her hands waving in animation. Tate listened with a smile on his face and then laughed.

Angela picked up the show program, scanned the next class. Jillie rode before she did. Great.

She put her braiding kit back in the trailer, checked the girth, then used a mounting block to swing herself into the saddle.

Five minutes later, she stood near the entrance to the ring. Jillie rode up, waited for the judge's nod, then entered the gate.

Tate stood on the other side of the entrance. Angela turned her horse and walked over.

"Hey," she said.

Tate glanced over his shoulder. "Hey."

"Isn't Jillie on Mrs. Mason's favorite?"

"Yeah," he said.

"I can't believe she's letting Jillie ride her."

"Guess she thinks she's ready for it," Tate said, his voice matter-of-fact.

Angela nodded, her gaze lingering on his face. Since the first day he'd walked into their school, she'd been completely taken. She was a movie fiend, and there wasn't a better-looking guy featured in any movie she'd ever seen.

Tate Callahan had light-blue eyes that looked as if they'd seen things that made him older than his sixteen years. His hair was on the long side, and his shoulders had started to widen on his lean body.

She looked at the ring where Jillie now cantered the perimeter and said with as little reluctance as she could muster, "They look good together."

"They do," he agreed, his gaze hanging on Jillie, as if she were every good thing he'd ever hoped for.

Another stab of jealousy riveted through her. What

was it about Jillie? She was more tomboy than girl. None of the other guys at school paid much attention to her. No one except Tate.

"If you want a job, you could work at our farm," she said, the words rushing out too fast so they ended up sounding a little desperate.

"Thanks, but I've got a job."

He responded without taking his eyes off Jillie. Angela's face burned red hot, and for the first time in her life, she had absolutely no idea how to go about getting what she wanted.

She turned her horse then and walked away, stopping a short distance back from the ring and watching Jillie finish her ride. When she was done, Tate met her at the exit gate, a big smile on his face. He unwrapped a piece of candy and gave it to the horse. Jillie smiled back at him, and Angela would have given up every single thing to which she'd been born just to be in her place.

10

Tate

I GET UP BEFORE the sun, sleep a wasted effort in my plain hotel room since I spent most of the night watching the numbers on the digital clock flip forward.

I pull my laptop computer from its case and stare at the blank screen, my fingers still against the keys.

Nothing.

I feel frozen inside. Locked up like an eighteen-wheeler careening down an ice-covered highway.

I slide back from the desk and slap the laptop closed, quickly getting dressed and packing my duffel bag before heading out of the room.

Few cars are out, as I drive down the quiet road leading to Westlake at just after six. I stop for coffee at Carter's, a small country store that hasn't changed much in the years since I left here, the paint a little more faded, the sign above the front door drooping a bit on the right side.

I park my car out front between two pickups with mud-spattered tires and jog up the steps, the front door dinging as I step inside.

A woman with bright-red hair and tired, blue eyes looks up from behind the cash register. "Morning."

"Morning," I say. "Coffee?"

"Just made some. First aisle on the left."

"Thanks."

Two men in overalls are talking by the coffee pot. I nod at them and pour a cup. I can feel the woman's gaze, as I pop a lid on the coffee and make my way back to the register.

"I know who you are," she says suddenly, clapping her hands together. A smile breaks across her face. "Tate Callahan. My goodness, in the flesh. I knew I recognized you, but it's sure been a long time. I didn't expect a real live celebrity to walk through the door at this hour of the day. You don't remember me, do you?"

I meet her wide-eyed gaze, sudden recognition flickering. "Alma Davis."

Color tints her cheeks, her smile growing wider. "We had algebra together."

I nod. "I remember."

"So what are you doing in these parts?" she asks with polite curiosity.

"I'm not sure, to be honest."

If she finds the answer odd, she doesn't let on. "I expect you got by to see Jillie, huh?"

"Yeah. I did," I say, handing her a five for the coffee.

She pops open the register, handing me my change. "You two used to be thick as thieves, if I remember right. Shame about her husband, wasn't it? Awfully young man to go that soon."

It takes a moment for the words to settle into

comprehension, and I stare at her for a moment, a cold sheen of sweat breaking across my skin. "What do you mean?"

"Jeffrey. He died last year. I assumed you knew—"

"What happened?" I ask, my voice not sounding like my own.

Alma shakes her head, red hair glancing her shoulders. "They say he committed suicide," she said, her voice lowering. "Hard to believe of someone who had all that he had. A wife, and those two little girls—"

I can hear the blood pounding in my ears now. "Girls?"

She leans back a bit, giving me a suspicious stare. "You must not have done much catching up with Jillie, after all," she says. "Kala and Corey."

Children. Jillie has children. I've never thought of her with children. Stupid, though. She's married. Had been married.

I remember then the things I said to her last night. Take that home to Jeffrey. I'm sure he'll be waiting to finish what I started.

I run a hand around the back of my neck, barely suppressing a groan.

"Would you mind signing my copy of your book?" Alma asks, pulling my thoughts back to the present. "I've read it twice, cover to cover. It's in the back, if you can hold on for a minute."

All I want is to get out of here. Sort through what I've just learned. But forcing a smile, I say, "Sure."

She's back in thirty seconds, handing me the book and waiting while I write something on the dedication page.

I scrawl a signature across the bottom, then hand back the pen and the book. "Real nice to see you, Alma."

"You, too, Tate. Come on back anytime."

I let myself out the door and take the steps to my car two at a time.

Backing out of the parking lot, I shove the stick shift into first and gun the car onto the two-lane road that leads out of town. I have to get out of here.

Jeffrey. Dead.

The words ricochet through me. Why hadn't Jillie told me last night?

As soon as the question surfaces, I ask myself why would she? I remember again the awful things I said to her, unwelcome remorse hot in my chest.

Just ahead on the right is the road that will take me back to US 220 and the interstate leading north. All I have to do is take the turn and head back to Manhattan and a life far removed from the memories this place brings back.

But I think of Jillie and the look on her face when she'd gotten out of the car last night. Considering our past, it shouldn't matter. I shouldn't care.

Which doesn't at all explain why just before reaching the interstate on-ramp, I slow the car and do a U-turn in the middle of the road, heading back and not away.

11

Jillie

I'VE JUST returned from taking the girls to school when there's a rap at my bedroom door.

Lucille sticks her head inside and says, "There's a call for you, Jillie."

The round-faced woman, who's worked some twenty years as a housekeeper for the Tailors, long ago won my heart when she refused to call me Jillian, as Judith had ordered her to.

"Who is it, Lucille?" I ask.

"He wouldn't give his name."

My stomach instantly drops. "Can you please tell him I'm not here?"

The older woman raises an eyebrow. "I already told him you were."

"Just tell him I'm . . . I don't know. Tell him I'm busy."

Lucille frowns. "Someday you have to start living again."

"Lucille. Please. Just tell him."

"All right," she says, shaking her head with a disapproving cluck.

I hear her pick up the extension in the hall outside the bedroom door. "I'm sorry, sir. She's busy," Lucille says, sounding as convincing as a deacon trying to explain to the pastor why he fell asleep during a Sunday sermon.

A moment later, Lucille reappears in the doorway. "He asked me to tell you he'll come over and wait until you're not too busy to see him."

If I had any doubt that it's Tate on the phone, I no longer do. "I'll take it in here."

Lucille smiles. "I'll just hang up here then," she says, disappearing from the room and closing the door behind her.

With damp palms, I pick up the phone beside the bed. "Hello."

"Can you meet me today?"

The voice is unmistakable, even though the anger that had tinted it the night before is now gone. "I think we already said everything we needed to say, Tate," I say, keeping my voice low.

"I don't think we did."

"Then we'll just have to agree to disagree."

"No one's living at Cross Country, right?"

"No. It's for sale," I say, feeling the same pang I feel every time I think of the farm I had loved so much.

"Meet me at the back pond in an hour. If you don't come, I'll see you at your front door," he says and hangs up before I can manage another word.

12

Jillie

I'M CLUTCHING THE steering wheel of the Mercedes so tightly that my knuckles are white against the dark leather.

I shouldn't have come. That would have been the right thing, the only thing that makes any sense. And yet, here I am, pulling up beside the black Porsche with my heart pounding so hard I have to lean my head against the back of the seat to steady my breathing.

This is no big deal. Really. A few words, and I'll be on my way. After all, what else is there to say?

I look out across the field to the pond where Tate now stands on the old dock, arms folded, his back to me. I feel a sudden catch in my throat, a deluge of old memories assaulting me.

How many summer afternoons had we lazed there in the sun, faces to the sky, pouring out our visions of the future? I would ride in the Olympics. Tate would be a famous writer.

At least one of us had made our dreams come true.

I force myself to open the door and get out. I stand for a moment, reaching for the courage to put one foot in front of the other and move.

He looks around then, and I stop as if I've been seared to the spot.

He lifts a hand and waves, and I am catapulted back to a time when we had been young, and just the sight of him weakened something deep inside me. It's unsettling to realize that the effect is the same.

I cross the grass field, setting my gaze to the right of him, and yet starkly aware that he watches me the entire way.

The dock has more creaks now than I remember. A few of the boards sag in places. A male and a female duck sit perched on the edge, diving into the water as I approach.

Tate stands a few feet away, his face serious and set. In the light of day, I can see that time has changed him. But if anything, it has only enhanced his appeal.

As a boy, he'd had the kind of looks that made perfectly intelligent girls forget their train of thought. The face that had once been boyish now has the planes and angles of a man, part of his appeal both then and now a noted indifference to the way he looks.

I glance down at the dock floor, aiming my voice at neutral. "What's the point of this, Tate?"

"An apology," he says quietly. "I owe you one."

"For?" I say, not quite able to hide my surprise.

"What I said last night. I'm sorry. I didn't know about Jeffrey."

I turn away from him, face the pond, watching the two ducks glide gracefully across the smooth surface. "Last night should not have happened."

He is silent for a moment, and then, "You're right. It shouldn't have."

The words are said with a humble honesty that brings back too many reminders of the Tate I had once known.

I look at him, see the intensity in his eyes, feeling something within me bend under its force.

We stand for a minute or more, awkwardness a vice encircling us both.

"Are you okay?" he asks finally.

Again, there is the old Tate in the question, concern at its core. I swallow hard, nod. I've kept everything that happened with Jeffrey locked up inside me, refusing to look at it or talk about it.

Tate is the friend I'd once confided in, as I have no other since.

The need to do so now feels too right, but with that rightness comes the full realization that he is not here to stay. That tomorrow, or the next day, he will be gone, and I will be left to figure out how to forget him again.

"I have to go," I say, turning to leave.

He stops me with a hand on my arm. "Jillie."

His voice on my name. Just that, and I have to close my eyes against a sudden onslaught of feeling. I don't say anything, but stand there, my feet refusing to move.

"Do you ever wish it had all worked out differently?" he asks.

I turn then, meeting the questions in his eyes. How can I answer? I have two wonderful daughters. For that and that alone, I could never regret the direction my life has taken.

Did I miss him?

Yes.

Do I still think about him?

Yes.

But I can say neither of these things now. There is nothing to be gained by it. "I have two incredible daughters," I say.

Another wash of silence before he says, "Were you happy with him?"

"I had every reason to be." I drop my chin, studying the boards beneath my feet. I look up then and find his gaze on me, steady and unwavering. It is the same as it had once been, his ability to see through whatever outside barriers I might have erected around myself. He had once known me, as no one else ever has, and the remembrance of that is there now, plain to see.

He waves a hand at the far end of the dock. "Sit a while?"

Refusal springs automatically to my lips. To stay is to extend something that has no place to go. I know this, and yet I find myself nodding, following him across the dock to the end that faces back toward Cross Country Farm.

He sits down, offers a hand for me to follow. I sit without taking it, feel his registration of the rebuff.

I look at him then, unable to turn away from his blue eyes. It's like it was before, this ability he has to see through me, inside to where the real truth lies. I feel as if he is looking for it now, trying to place something he missed.

I put my gaze straight ahead and say, "It's sad, seeing this place empty."

"What happened?"

"The Masons sold it a few years ago. They bought another farm in Florida and retired there. Apparently, the new owners purchased the place as an investment and haven't done anything with it. It's for sale again. Someone said if it doesn't go pretty quickly, they're tearing down the house and barn and building some kind of housing development."

"That would be a shame," he says.

I lift a shoulder in resignation, trying for an indifference I don't feel. "Things change, I guess."

"Do you still ride?" he asks.

I shake my head.

"Why? You lived for it."

"Other directions, I guess."

"You giving up horses? That's something I really can't imagine."

Just the words send up an intense spear of longing. Not just for riding, but for the map of my life I had once so believed in and shared with Tate.

How can I tell him that for all these years I've been trying to fit myself into a mold I finally realized I would never fit in? And in trying to fix what I'd broken, I'd ruined everything.

I get to my feet, quickly, stumble back a step. "I have to go," I say.

He stands, shoving his hands in the pockets of his faded jeans, the stance so reminiscent of the boy he had been that I have to look away. "What are you running from, Jillie?" he asks.

"I'm not running," I say. "But I won't deny that this is painful. And pointless. I really am happy for you, Tate. And proud of you, too. You've done everything you said you were going to. At least one of us did."

I turn then and run across the grass, not looking back, even as I get inside the Mercedes and drive away.

13

Tate

I SIT ON the dock for a long time after she leaves.

She's right. Everything has changed. And yet it seems as if the life we led together couldn't have been more than a blink ago. All those plans we made. Dreams we put into words and shared with each other.

In the years since I left the lake, I've kept it all locked away, never let myself go anywhere near what might have been. Those are dangerous waters, and I simply never let myself sail in them.

But being here. . .seeing her. . .that is something different altogether.

For so long, anger has been the stake I drove through the heart of whatever memories I had of Jillie. It worked too. That anger ran deep. Led me to write a book that, ironically enough, gave me a career I had always wanted.

Jillie was the first person who ever believed in me. I've let myself forget that. I remember it now, though, the acknowledgment piercing through me with a sharp arrow.

We had once been everything to each other. Compass, divining rod. I'd never had anyone look at me the way Jillie looked at me then. As if I were the rainbow and the pot of gold, all in one.

And, if I'm honest with myself, no one has ever made me want to live up to the possibility, before or since.

When We Were Sixteen

"DO YOU EVER write about your feelings?"

I looked up from the notebook into which I'd been writing fast and hard. Jillie studied me with interested eyes.

I shook my head. "Guys don't write about stuff like that."

"Why not?"

"Too girly."

"Girly!"

"Jane Austen and Emily Dickinson stuff."

Jillie laughed. "If you don't write about feelings, what do you write about?"

"Fights, car races, shootouts."

She rolled her eyes. "Oh, there's some interesting stuff."

We were in the horse barn at Cross Country, up in the hayloft, sitting on the wood floor, our backs against a stack of orchard-grass hay just put up that spring. Its sweet aroma filled the air, and I thought, not for the first time, that I could live in this barn. Jillie and I spent every free moment there, riding for Mrs. Mason, or just hanging around when we were done.

"When are you going to let me read it?" Jillie asked now.

"Never."

"Why not?"

"Nobody's ever read it."

"So how are you going to be a famous writer, if you never let anybody read your work?"

He lifted a shoulder. "Someday I will."

"No time like the present." She grabbed for the book, yanked it from me, and scrambled across the floor on hands and knees, the spiral binder clutched between her teeth.

"Hey, Jillie, come back here!"

"Gotta catch me first!" She was up and running then to the far end of the loft, climbing a stack of hay bales.

I went after her, full throttle. I caught her by the leg of her jeans, but she yanked free, laughing and climbing higher.

At the top of the stack, I tackled her, and we both rolled, stopping just short of the edge. I straddled her, pinning her beneath me. She held the notebook up high, reading the words out loud.

"Her hair is like sunshine, her smile the brightest day of summer—"

I yanked it from her hand, but it was too late. She was staring at me, her eyes wide, her lips parting, but no sound came out.

I flung the notebook over my shoulder. It slid down the stacked hay and landed on the aisle floor far below with a thump.

"Why'd you do that?" she asked, the words soft.

"You shouldn't have read it."

"I'm sorry," she said, serious now. "Really, Tate. I am."

I stared down at her, the heat that stayed on constant simmer when I was with her, now blazing high and wide.

And suddenly, I wasn't thinking about the blasted notebook anymore. Or my own embarrassment. All I could think about was Jillie and how she felt beneath me.

Every curve, every contour, and I wanted to map the feel of her in my mind so that I could remember when I was alone again, wishing I were with her.

It was one of those hot summer afternoons when the air was completely still. A bee buzzed somewhere above us, the sound amplified in my ears. Outside, the tractor was going, and in the stalls below, one of the horses thumped a wall with a shoe.

"Tate," she said, her voice raspy.

"Yeah?"

"Would you please kiss me?"

This didn't sound like the Jillie of a few minutes ago. Gone was the teasing, and in its place something that I'd never heard before. A yearning that echoed my own feelings.

From the first day I'd come to live at Smith Mountain Lake, my only plan had been to leave as fast as I could. A string of foster homes had taught me early on that you couldn't count on anyone in this world except yourself. I'd been let down enough times to know my theory held water.

But Jillie was different. It was as if we'd been made to go together, like two sides of a single coin. When I was with her, the world made sense, had direction and purpose.

And somewhere along the way, I'd started to think that maybe I didn't have to do it all by myself, more important, that I didn't want to.

Looking down at her, I wanted to kiss her more than I'd ever wanted anything in my life. "Are you sure, Jillie?"

"If I get any more sure," she said, "I'm going to die of it."

I lowered my head then, hovered just above her mouth. She raised up, and our lips brushed. Feeling jolted through me, and I wasn't sure who leaned in next, her or me, but suddenly we were kissing like we'd been doing it all our lives.

Instantly, I understood why people wrote songs about this, why guys in the locker room talked about it like they just discovered another part of the world where no one had ever been before.

Once, when I was thirteen, I'd kissed a girl, or more like, she'd kissed me. Poppy Sullivan had cornered me one night after summer Bible school when I came out of the church restroom. I never told Jillie about that kiss, and even now, I wasn't sure why. Except that it hadn't been anything like I'd hoped kissing would be – it was a dry, hard peck that made me wonder what all the fuss was about.

I thought maybe now I knew. If it wasn't with someone who made you feel the way I felt around Jillie, then it wasn't any big deal at all.

She put her arms around my neck then and pulled me down. I stretched out across her, and it felt like coming home ought to feel, that sense of being in the right place, a place of belonging.

We opened our mouths to each other, and I deepened the kiss. She made a soft, pleased sound that made me wish we could stay up here for the rest of our lives.

She put her hands on my face, and said, "You know how long I've been waiting for you to do that?"

"How long?" I asked, not recognizing my own hoarse voice.

"Practically since the first day we met."

I wondered then what she saw in me, something no one else ever had for sure. Whatever it was, it made me want to move mountains for her, give her every good thing the world had to offer. "The very first day?" I said, reaching for a light note and failing.

"Very first."

We stared at each other for a long time, maybe both of us deciding that it was okay to let the other one see what we felt.

"Jillie! You in here?"

Marshall Andrews' voice rang out from the center aisle below.

"Your dad," I said, dropping down beside her, my arm curved around her shoulders. I looked up at the rafters and tried counting the beams, anything to slow my pounding heart. "Shouldn't you answer?" I whispered.

"And what am I going to say?" she whispered back.

"That you're up here in the hayloft kissing me, and you'll be right down?"

She bit back a giggle, and we wrestled our clothes back into place.

"I'll go down," I said. "You stay up here."

I took the ladder to the aisle, feeling Jillie's father's eyes on my back the entire way. I dropped onto the concrete floor and tried to look surprised to see him.

Mr. Andrews stood with my notebook in his hand. "This yours?" he asked.

"Yes, sir," I said, praying he hadn't read it.

"Have you seen Jillie?"

"Yes, sir," I said, refusing to lie to him. Marshall Andrews had given me my job at Cross Country, taken a chance on me when every other place I'd applied for a summer job had turned me down as soon as they saw that I was a foster kid. "She's around here somewhere, sir."

Mr. Andrews handed me the notebook without letting go of my gaze. "I expect she is," he said, and I had no doubt he knew exactly where she was. "The tractor's got a flat. Give me a hand?"

"Sure thing," I said, following him down the aisle.

Just before I got to the main door, I glanced back up at the loft where Jillie sat on a bale of hay, knees drawn up against her chest. And in her smile was all the promise I'd never imagined I could begin to hope for.

14

Jillie

TONIGHT IS ONE of the rare nights when I have the house to myself with the girls. Judith had left earlier to have dinner with her sister, and Angela slipped out shortly after without saying where she was going.

For the past hour, I've been helping Corey study for a spelling test. We sit at the kitchen table, me at one end, Corey at the corner. At the other end, Kala sits with her Algebra book open, a pencil in her hand.

I call out the next word. "Intuitive."

"That's a hard one," Corey says, fiddling with one of her pigtails.

"Sound it out," I remind her.

"In-tu-it-ive."

"Good. So now spell it."

"I n t u e—"

"You're hopeless," Kala says, rolling her eyes.

"Kala," I say, giving her a stern look.

"Well, it's true," Kala shoots back. "You help her every

night, and she still can't spell worth a darn." She shoves her chair back and bolts up from the table, storming out the back door of the kitchen.

I lean over and kiss Corey on the top of her head. "I'll be right back, honey. Practice the next couple without me."

"Okay, Mommy."

I stop at the kitchen door, looking out across the back yard. Kala sits at the base of an old oak, arms wrapped around her knees, her head turned away from the house. I open the screen door, walk across the yard and sit down next to her.

"Do you want to tell me what that was all about?"

Kala folds her arms, refusing to look at me. "Nothing, Mom."

I pull a blade of grass, rubbing it between thumb and forefinger. "You can tell me, you know."

Kala drops her gaze, tracing a finger through the dirt at the base of the tree. "Why do we still live here?"

The question catches me by surprise. For a moment, I can't think of a response. "This was your father's home, honey."

"Yeah, and he's gone, so why do we stay?"

I'm a little taken aback by the hardness in Kala's voice and at the same time hit with the sudden feeling that a trap door waits beneath my answer. "Has something happened, Kala?"

She bites her lip, looking down at the ground. "Nothing different."

"What does that mean, honey?"

Another stretch of silence, and then, "It means that Grandma criticizes everything I do. My clothes are never right. My hair's too long. I have on the wrong shoes. I know I'm not as pretty as Corey, but does she have to remind me of it every single day?"

I feel as if I've been doused with a bucket of cold water. The passion behind my daughter's words gives credence to the fact that the feelings are not new. I put a hand on her shoulder, wanting to pull her into my arms, but feeling her resistance. "Honey, I'm sure she doesn't mean—"

"She does mean it, Mom!" she says, interrupting. "Why else would she say it?" Kala jumps to her feet, running across the yard and back into the house.

I start to go after her, but make myself stay put. How can I tell her the reason? How can I risk the very real possibility that she might never forgive me?

The screen door opens, then shuts. Corey troops across the yard, plopping down on her knees beside me.

"Are you okay, Mommy?"

I reach out and smooth wavy, blonde hair back from her face. "Yes," I say.

"What's wrong with Kala?" she asks with unusual seriousness.

I struggle for the right words. "She's going through kind of a hard time right now."

"She sure is grouchy."

"Sometimes when we're upset about something, we act a certain way, and we really don't mean to. Things will get better, honey."

Corey snuggles up in my arms, putting her head against my chest. From my youngest child, I feel complete and utter trust. She believes my words, and, in that moment, I want nothing more than to prove myself worthy of this.

But the truth is I don't know if I am.

15

Angela

AT JUST AFTER eight, Angela slides into the booth of her regular table at Miller's, a dinner spot set in a quiet cove of the lake that draws people by both boat and car.

The place is hopping tonight. The bar vibrates with liquor bottles clinking against glasses, flirtatious laughter echoing above the Top 40 tunes playing from a set of booming speakers while the band sets up.

A young waitress with a sleek ponytail and red lipstick stops by the table and asks for her order. "Bombay and tonic," she says.

"Be right back with that."

Angela rarely drinks. She finds the effects of alcohol more aggravating than invigorating. But after another day of problems for which she doesn't have answers, she feels in need of a lift. Sometimes, it seems as if her feet are stuck in quicksand, and pull as she might, she cannot free herself.

"Hey!"

She looks up to find Poppy Sullivan sliding into the booth beside her, a huge smile on her face.

"You're disgusting," Angela says. "How can you look so cheerful after the day we just had?"

"I get off on problems," she says, smiling. "You've got to change your outlook. Reframe it, that's all."

"Clearly, there's something wrong with you."

Poppy laughs with an elegant shrug, dropping her Kate Spade purse on the seat beside her. "So what's new?"

It is this that Angela envies most about Poppy. They've been friends since grade school. Had she so chosen, Poppy could have spent her twenties on the cover of Vogue. Nearly six feet tall, she is one of those women for whom clothes appear to be made and the rest of the female population mourns their inability to wear.

But Poppy's other asset is a keen intelligence that she puts to daily use as a vice-president at TaylorMade Industries. Angela is the first to admit that without Poppy this past year, she would have sunk beneath the weight of her own mistakes.

"So I stopped for some smokes on the way over. You'll never guess what I ran across."

The waitress arrives with Angela's drink. Poppy asks for a glass of water.

Angela takes a sip of her gin and tonic. "What?"

Poppy opens her purse, pulling out a folded newspaper. She unfolds it and hands it to Angela.

Angela's gaze falls across the front page. The photo she received by e-mail jumps out at her again, making her sit back in her seat and draw in a quick breath. The headline accompanying it sends a sick feeling trickling through her chest to settle in a solid lump at the pit of her stomach.

"Is this a joke?" she finally rasps in a voice that doesn't sound like her own.

Poppy smiles. "Could I make stuff like this up?"

The answer is most likely yes, but it doesn't appear to be true in this case. "Who. . .how did they get this picture?"

"You didn't give it to them?" The question comes out sounding half like a joke, half not.

"Of course I didn't!"

Poppy holds up a perfectly manicured hand. "Whoa. Just teasing, hon."

"It's not funny. This must be somebody's idea of a sick joke," Angela says, her hands suddenly shaky.

"It couldn't be doing anything for Tate's new career."

Angela, of course, knows of Tate's success. He'd become the lake's poster boy for wrong-side-of-the-tracks makes it to the big time.

She glances at the article again. Who would dig all this up?

Jillie? She doesn't think so. Jillie has her own cracked heart to deal with where Tate Callahan is concerned.

So, who? And why?

She runs a hand through her hair. "What if my mother sees this?"

"She'll have a heart attack," Poppy says. "But then maybe that wouldn't be such a bad thing?"

Angela shoots her friend a sharp glance. Sometimes, it is hard to tell when Poppy is joking and when she isn't.

Needing a moment to herself, Angela says, "Be right back," then heads for the ladies' room.

For once, it is empty. She stands before the white bowl sink, studying herself in the mirror. She looks shell-shocked, her eyes wide and alarmed, her cheeks flushed with color.

She turns on the faucet, leans over and splashes cold water on her face. The shock feels good. She reaches for a paper towel, dabs her skin dry, then anchors one hand to the sink, as if without it she might topple over.

Do old sins really come back to haunt?

The question is one she doesn't want to know the answer to. She wheels around and flies out of the bathroom, crashing head on into a wide chest.

"Whoa there."

"I'm sorry," she says, embarrassment heating her face.

"No problem."

The amused voice belongs to a thirty-something man with blond hair that touches the collar of his shirt, white cotton with a torn pocket. His eyes have crinkles at the corners, as if he laughs a lot. It occurs to her that he looks like a young Jon Bon Jovi.

Angela takes a couple of steps back, her gaze still snagging with his.

"You gonna hang around?" he asks. "We're getting ready to play."

"Oh. You're with—"

"The band," he finishes, smiling again.

"I, yes," she says, feeling a sudden flush of color. "Probably."

"That's good. Okay."

The smile that accompanies the statement belongs to a guy who knows his way around girls. The kind of girls who know how to flirt back, get a seat up front where he can sing directly to them. Angela isn't one of those girls, never has been, most likely never will be. Too bad Poppy isn't the one bumping into him.

She'd know what to do with a guy like this.

Angela drops her gaze, runs a hand through her hair. "I'd better get back to my table."

"I'll be looking for you," he says, and disappears inside the men's room.

Angela feels the heat of his smile all the way to the table.

"What's with the look?" Poppy says.

"What look?" Angela shakes her head, trying to sound clueless.

"Like you just got caught in a pair of headlights."

"Just some guy on the way out of the bathroom."

"Must have been hot," Poppy says.

"Too hot for me."

"Sounds like exactly what you need."

"I'll leave that to you."

Just then, the band members start gathering on stage. The drummer taps a snare, doing a practice roll. Two guys with guitars and shoulder-length hair strum a warm-up.

The young Bon Jovi joins them, and Angela feels a catch in her chest just looking at him. He is gorgeous, young, fit, with muscles that ripple beneath his white T-shirt. Faded blue jeans encase well-shaped legs, and it occurs to her that she has never been out with someone like him before.

Her dates are the country-club type, khaki pants and golf shirts, all Judith preapproved.

Thirty-six years old, and she has never been out with anyone who doesn't meet her mother's stamp of standard.

Poppy leans forward, putting a hand on Angela's arm. "Is that the guy?"

Angela pulls her gaze from the stage, taking a sip of her now watery gin and tonic. "Yeah. No big deal."

Poppy tips her head, giving him a thorough perusal. "Oh, I'd have to disagree with that. He's a big deal."

"Not my type."

"Maybe you ought to change your type," Poppy says.

The singer picks up the mike, says hello to the audience. People begin clapping, whistling. He smiles and tucks into a number that brings couples crowding to the dance floor.

He turns then, looks directly at Angela, and winks. For a moment, she is sure he must have intended that for Poppy. But he is looking at her. Straight on. She thinks about what Poppy said and wishes suddenly that she could do exactly that. Change her type.

Unfortunately, like everything else in her life, it has been chosen for her.

16

Poppy

POPPY STAYS LONG after Angela leaves. Ridiculous for a thirty-six year-old woman to have a curfew, but under Judith Taylor's roof, rules are rules.

Poppy leans back in the booth, summons a waitress for the drink she refused when Angela was here.

A firm believer in staying on her toes, Poppy never drinks when she has a mission to carry out. And tonight's mission had gone beautifully. The look on Angela's face at the sight of that rag paper. What she would have given for a snapshot.

A guy in a Harley-Davidson T-shirt and black jeans approaches her table. "Hey," he says.

She looks up at him, does a quick appraisal. "Hey, yourself."

"You all by your lonesome?"

"By choice," she says, tapping a nail on the table.

"Any chance I could get a shot at changing your mind?"

He is better than passably good-looking, black hair, blue eyes, but unfortunately, that and that alone won't do. Poppy has standards, and anything that falls short of them, well, she isn't interested.

She learned a long time ago that there is only one way someone like her gets ahead in life. Chart a course, and don't deviate.

"Thanks," she says, "but what would be the point?"

His eyes widen at the question. "I can think of a few points."

"I'm sure you can," she says. "Not interested."

He raises a hand, backs away.

Poppy watches him walk to the bar, shake his head at something another guy nursing a beer says to him.

Too bad. In some ways, she's just like Angela. Someone her age shouldn't have to live such a restricted life. But there is too much to be lost by a wrong choice.

The band gears up for its last set. The lead singer glances at her table, flashing a look of disappointment at Angela's empty seat. How sweet, Poppy thinks. Maybe she'll just have to cheer him up.

Ordinarily, she wouldn't have given a guy in a band a second look, but then Angela had preapproved him, after all.

And anything Angela wants, well, Poppy wants it more.

Elementary School

POPPY SULLIVAN WAS born Prudence Elizabeth to parents who barely had two nickels to rub together.

Her father served as the pastor at Second Baptist Church in a poor part of the county, where most of the houses had broken-down cars in the front yards as lawn ornamentation. The parsonage in which they lived was a cleaned-up version of that, a smaller-than-small brick ranch within spitting distance of the church itself.

Like the house, her parents were plainer than plain. Early on, Poppy understood that there was something unusual about a child who looked like her, being born to people who looked like her parents. The more discreet members of her father's congregation declared him a man blessed by God to have such a lovely daughter. Less than tactful members, like Lillian Overstreet, whom no one wanted to sit behind on Sundays because of her haystack hairdo, asked if she was adopted.

For the first few years of her life, Poppy was a happy child: content was the word her mother used to describe her. Poppy thought of those years as the ones during which she hadn't known how the rest of the world lived.

All that changed at age seven when she received an invitation to Angela Taylor's birthday party.

Poppy's birthdays had been celebrated with a cake her mother made and a present or two selected from the wide array of plastic available at the Dollar General store.

"There are children in this world who will never have a toy, Poppy," her mother always said. "I think it's a far better thing for you to have a less-expensive present and give the rest to the Lottie Moon offering. Down the road, you'll feel so much more gratification for having done that than you would for another doll to sit on your bed."

Poppy disagreed, but her mother was a woman of strong convictions, and once she made up her mind about something, it did little good to try to change it.

It was also Angela's birthday party that opened her

eyes to the fact that other children weren't donating their presents to Lottie Moon.

Her dad drove her to the Taylor house, a mansion by any standards Poppy could imagine. It looked like something out of those *Southern Living* magazines her mother checked out of the library to copy recipes she wanted to try.

Her dad let her out at the front door and waited while Poppy rang the bell. When a large woman in a black and white maid's uniform opened the door and beckoned her in with a smile, he drove away.

The woman led her down an enormous hallway and through a kitchen bigger than Poppy's whole house. Just outside lay a beautiful pool with water so blue it didn't look real. A dozen or more kids jumped off the diving board, throwing a beach ball back and forth.

Poppy looked down at the frilly, pink dress her mother had made her, felt her cheeks flame as bright as her hair.

She hadn't known she was supposed to bring a swimsuit.

Just then Angela got out of the pool and trotted over. They were in first grade together, but they'd never actually said much to each other.

"I like your dress," Angela said.

Poppy tried to smile, unable to decide whether Angela was being kind or cruel. "Thank you," she said.

"Did you bring a bathing suit?"

Poppy shook her head.

"I bet you could wear one of mine. Come on," she said, taking Poppy by the hand and tugging her toward a gazebo that turned out to be a changing room.

No fewer than ten bathing suits hung on a rack, some with the tags still on.

"Which one do you like?" Angela asked.

Poppy studied them, then pointed to a green one. "Is that one okay?"

"Sure. And it'll look great with your hair."

They went outside, and Angela jumped back in the pool, waving for Poppy to join her. Her father had taught her to swim last summer at the YMCA. She was now grateful for those lessons.

Angela stuck by Poppy's side for the rest of the party. Maybe she felt sorry for her. If so, it didn't matter. Poppy wanted to know everything there was to know about her. What it was like to live in a house like this every day of your life. How amazing it must be to have your own pool and invite friends over any time you wanted to.

When it was time to go, all the children lined up at the front door. Mrs. Taylor stood beside them and spoke to each of the parents as they picked up their child. Suddenly, Poppy was aware of how much older her father's car was than the other cars there. She could see him several vehicles back in line, and she wished suddenly that she could have caught a ride with one of the other families.

Finally, it was her turn, and her father's old Nova pulled up to the door. It had a huge rust spot on the passenger side, and the muffler made an awful, rattling sound, smoke pouring from it.

Poppy's cheeks burned as she got in, feeling the eyes of the other children on her.

They drove down the driveway, and Poppy turned to look back at the big house. Angela stood at the door, waving at her, as if she were truly sorry to see her go.

"Did you have fun, honey?" her father asked.

"It was nice," she said, unable to quit thinking about

everything she'd seen. The enormous rooms, so many of them they couldn't possibly be used all the time. The swimming pool in the backyard. The lady in the black and white maid's uniform who had served them lemonade and cookies.

"Daddy?"

"Yes, honey?"

"Why don't we have a big house like the Taylors?"

Her father didn't answer for a moment, as if he were looking for exactly the right thing to say. "God has been good to them, Poppy; but He's been good to us too."

Poppy wondered if her dad really believed that. If that was why it had taken him so long to answer. She stared out the window. Couldn't he see how much better God had been to the Taylors? She wanted to ask him why, but didn't. Maybe why didn't matter. But from that moment, there was one thing she did know. She wasn't willing to accept her father's lot in life.

A person could be something other than what they were born into.

Poppy had every intention of proving it.

17

Tate

I CAN'T SLEEP.

It's after four o'clock, and I've yet to close my eyes. I get out of bed and pull a bottle of water from the mini-bar next to the TV.

My laptop sits on the desk by the window, the lid closed. I flip it open, sit down, and stare at the screen until dawn ducks into the room, the rising sun throwing light across the hotel's carpeted floor.

In frustration, I shrug into running clothes and head out of the building, across the parking lot and onto a two-lane road. I follow it to the edge of Westlake, running three miles or so along the road and then doubling back.

On mile four, I start to break a good sweat. I kick up the pace of the fifth mile, slowing to cool down just as I reach Westlake again.

New businesses are interspersed with the old ones I remember. A new dry cleaners sits next to the old bakery.

The smells drifting from the open front door of the bakery make my mouth water.

Just down from there, a cupcake place and a hardware store have taken up residence. Kay's Kafe sits a little farther down. When I lived here, it was the local place to go for a good homecooked meal. From the outside, it has changed little.

By now, a cup of coffee sounds good. Inside, most of the tables are taken. I grab the morning paper and make my way to the far corner of the diner.

A waitress in khaki pants and a white blouse approaches with a pot of coffee. She has tamed her curly, red hair into a ponytail and looks out at me over a pair of glasses that sit low on her nose. "Pour you a cup?"

"Please," I say.

She leaves me with a menu and promises to be right back.

I take a sip of the hot coffee and open the paper. It's filled with small town news – chamber of commerce meeting the first Monday of the month, the local humane society to host a benefit on the following Saturday.

I think of the borrowed apartment in Manhattan, the Airstream trailer I've been calling home the past couple of years.

Something about it suddenly seems lacking to me now.

I order the special: scrambled eggs and toast with a glass of orange juice. The plate arrives within minutes, and I tuck into it with an appetite I haven't felt in a long time. I hear my name from a few tables away, look up to see three men staring at me.

One of the men gets up, walks over. He's wearing navy coveralls and a Reynolds' Tire cap. "Well, well," he says. "Never thought I'd see you around here again."

I recognize him then. Todd Bendermier is an older version of the boy I went to school with, the sneer on his face the most recognizable of his features. He's put on thirty pounds, mostly around his midsection.

"Surprised myself," I say.

"It must have taken a lot of courage to come back. Knowing you wouldn't be welcome, I mean."

"Somebody make you the greeting committee?"

Todd laughs an unamused laugh. "Unofficially."

"If it's unofficial, I guess it doesn't count."

"Still don't know how to take a hint, do you, Callahan?"

"You want to spell it out for me?"

"Be glad to. We don't like your kind around here. Didn't when you came here before. Still don't."

"I'll be sure to file that under Important Stuff to Remember," I say.

Todd gives me a narrow glare, tips his hat, and walks back to his table.

The group leaves a few minutes later, a clatter of boots on the restaurant's wood floor.

I finish looking at the paper, drink another cup of coffee. The waitress brings the check, telling me to stay as long as I like.

But the encounter with Todd reminds me of what it is like to be an outsider, to live in a place where I don't really belong. I drop a ten on the table, put the paper back on the front counter and leave.

Outside, the sun has lifted higher in the sky, and the sounds of early morning fill the air. A big truck in the distance, a church bell tolling eight o'clock.

I head back toward the hotel. Hearing footsteps behind me, I glance over my shoulder.

They come at me at once, shoving me into a space between two brick buildings in a group tackle. My right shoulder hits the asphalt, taking the weight of the fall.

I roll. A hard boot kicks me in the stomach. The air leaves my lungs in a whoosh. Another boot lands a blow to my shoulder. Blackness sucks at the light. I blink hard, try to stand.

"You left here once. Shoulda kept it that way."

A fist connects with my jaw, hurling me backwards. I lie there on the pavement, my gaze locked on the strip of blue sky wedged between the buildings.

Laughter ricochets like bullets. I raise my head and try to look at their faces, but can't focus.

The blue sky above me narrows to a thin line, then disappears altogether.

18

Jillie

THE MORNING STARTS off much as the night ended.

Kala isn't talking, and Corey tags along behind her like a contrite puppy seeking forgiveness, even though she has no idea what she did wrong.

I've just dropped them off at school when my cell phone rings. I stop behind a bus waiting to pull out onto the main road and pick it up.

"Hey, Jillie, it's Linda Saunders. Lucille gave me your number. Hope that was all right."

Linda and I are in the same women's group at church. She's an emergency-room nurse at the hospital, and while we aren't exactly friends, we've had a few conversations over coffee. "Of course," I say.

"You can do with this what you want, but we had a patient brought in this morning. I think you know him. Tate Callahan?"

I sit back in my seat, surprise knocking the breath from me. "Yes. What happened?"

"He's been beaten up pretty badly. A cracked shoulder. Lot of bruises."

"Is he all right?"

"I think he will be. But he's been admitted. He said there wasn't anyone to call. I remembered that you two were good friends growing up. I just thought—"

"Thank you, Linda," I say. "I appreciate you calling."

"Sure," she says. "See you soon."

I click off the phone, wondering what I'm supposed to do with this. A car behind me honks. I glance up. The bus has disappeared. I drive on.

A quarter mile or so and I pull over, leaning my head on the steering wheel.

Someone beat up Tate? I have no idea what to think of this, much less what to do, if anything.

What good would it do for me to see him? We aren't a part of each other's lives anymore.

There wasn't anyone to call.

Linda's words echo back. Tate has no real family. Maybe we don't know each other anymore. But we did once, and shouldn't that count for something?

19

Tate

I OPEN MY eyes to the glare of a fluorescent light. I stare up at it, trying to figure out where I am.

The answer hits me at the same time that awareness of pain steamrolls over me. Everything hurts. I can't differentiate between the locations, as if my body is under assault from one huge, pounding ache.

"Hey."

I jerk my gaze to the side of the bed. Jillie. I close my eyes. "What are you doing here?"

"I could ask the same of you," she says.

I force myself to look at her again. "What time is it?"

"One-thirty."

"How did I—"

"They said the rescue squad brought you in. That you'd been beaten up."

Memory hits then. The alley. The three guys taking me down. I suppress a groan. "You didn't have to come here."

"No, I didn't," she says.

There is something of the old Jillie in her voice, and I make an effort to bring her into focus. She stands, pours me a cup of water from the plastic pitcher on the table next to the bed. I try to reach for it, dropping back onto the pillow as another wave of pain assaults me.

"Here," she says. "Let me help." She puts her hand behind my head, brings the cup to my lips.

The water tastes like heaven. I swallow several times, then lie back on the pillow. "Thank you."

"You're welcome. Are you uncomfortable?"

"A little," I say. Actually, it feels as if I have a knife embedded in too many parts of my body to count.

Something of that must have shown on my face because she says, "I'll be right back."

She returns a couple of minutes later with a pleasant-faced nurse who clucks and says, "You should have pushed your call button, Mr. Callahan. No sense in lying here miserable. I'll fix you right up."

She picks up my IV tubing, inserts a syringe, and injects medication into the line, "You should feel better in a few minutes."

I nod. "Thank you."

"You call me when you need me, okay? My name's on the board there. Mrs. Walters."

She leaves the room in a hurry, as if she knows she's needed elsewhere. I lie still, the drug like a blanket cloaking me in comfort.

Jillie stands by the window, her back to me, arms folded.

"Jillie."

She turns and looks at me.

"Thanks for coming," I say.

20

Jillie

THE GIRLS HAVE dance class on Wednesday afternoons, so I won't be picking them up until five.

Tate has been asleep for two-and-a-half hours. Hospital sounds echo in the hallway, carts rolling by, nurses speaking in soft voices. I sit in a chair next to the bed and listen to him breathe, watch him with the luxury of being able to take my fill.

There are lines on his face where there had once been none, but they add character, something I somehow knew, when we were kids, that age would bring to his appearance. He is lean and muscled, his dark-brown hair short, the way he wore it as a boy, too impatient to do anything more than run a comb through it.

A bruise has begun to sprout beneath his left eye, blue black. Large, white bandages cover both his hands and his right forearm, dried blood visible at the edges. Evidence of fighting back, which, of course, he would.

I want to put my hand over his, draw out the pain that

must surely burn there. I think of how once I would have done exactly that.

With this thought, I stand abruptly, walk to the window, and stare out at the parking lot below. A group of doctors in white coats cross the sidewalk, disappearing inside the building. Maybe I should go. Maybe staying isn't a good idea.

"You're still here."

I jump at his voice, turn to find him studying me through serious eyes.

I cross back to the bed. "How are you feeling?"

"Better."

"Good." I hesitate, awkward. "Can I get you anything?"

"Thanks," he says. "I'm fine."

I sit down in the chair, my legs feeling as if I've just climbed a dozen flights of stairs. "Who did this, Tate?"

He shakes his head. "It doesn't matter."

I try not to look disapproving. "How can it not matter?"

"It doesn't matter for now."

"You do know. Have you told the police?"

"Only that I didn't know who they were."

"Is that true?"

He doesn't answer me, as if he doesn't want to put voice to the lie.

"You never were any good at letting someone help you."

"I don't need help with this one," he says.

"They're not worth the effort. They put you in the hospital, Tate. Let the police take care of it."

He's quiet for a long string of moments, before he says, "Life has a way of eventually dealing any cards that need to be dealt. And besides I doubt they're feeling so great right now, either." A hint of a smile touches his mouth. "I gave as good as I got."

"I don't doubt that a bit."

21

Tate

LONG AFTER JILLIE leaves, I stare at the ceiling, the drug from earlier having worn off enough that I feel the throb of pain in a half-dozen different places.

Without Jillie's presence, the room feels like what it is, a strange place where I am alone.

It's not as if I don't know the feeling. Most of my life, I've been exactly that. I wonder what it would be like to have family to call, people who would come by and bring chocolate chip cookies and extra clothes.

For me, that would have once been Jillie.

Ironic that she had been the only person here today.

I glance down at my bandage-covered hands. Realize I haven't even considered what this means for my book deadline.

Todd is the same blockhead he'd been during school, but that doesn't make it any easier to take his insults.

I don't care what other people think. As long as I know the truth, what difference does it make?

But then, all it takes is one sleazy article in a sleazy tabloid, and people start seeing you through someone else's lense.

I left this place with other peoples' lies settling like a fog around me, through which no one cared to look for the truth. I realize suddenly that in leaving, maybe I validated those lies.

I'm awake for a long time after the lights in the hall are dimmed and the nurses' voices lower to whispers. I think about the fact that I'd driven down here with the intention of confronting Jillie about the article and then getting the hell back out again.

But something is suddenly too clear to ignore. I'm not leaving this place again until it's on my own terms. Before I go, I will know the truth about what happened all those years ago. And so will everyone else.

22

Jillie

AFTER I TAKE Kala and Corey to school the next morning, I tell myself there is no point in going back to the hospital. Tate has everything he needs. What can I really do?

This does not explain then why I am turning into the hospital parking lot a few minutes later, or why I make my way through the double glass doors and take the elevator to his room.

I knock at the door. When there is no answer, I stick my head inside.

The bed is empty. Before I can weigh the significance of that, the bathroom door opens, and Tate steps out, freshly shaved, his wet hair combed back from his ridiculously good-looking face.

He glances up, looking more than a little surprised to see me. "Hey," he says.

"Hey," I say, feeling awkward. "How are you?"

"I'll live."

"Improved, I take it."

He looks at me for a moment and says, "You didn't have to come back."

I lift a shoulder. "I know."

"I'm sure you have plenty of other things to do. Children and all."

I wish I could say yes, my day is planned to the minute, chock full of meaningful events, one right after the other. But the next meaningful thing on my list will be picking up Kala and Corey at three o'clock. "I thought you might need a ride back to your car. Although, I guess you won't be driving with your hands like that."

"No," he says. "I guess I won't. Not for a few days anyway."

The door opens, and the same nurse from yesterday bustles in. "I see you're all ready to go, Mr. Callahan. And someone here to pick you up at that."

Tate looks at me.

"Yes," I say.

The nurse rolls a wheelchair inside. "If you're ready then, I'll chauffeur you downstairs."

"I'll be fine to walk," he says.

"Hospital policy," she says, patting the chair.

He obliges with obvious reluctance. Downstairs, I pull the car up to the front door where the smiling nurse waits with Tate. She insists on helping him into the passenger side and also assisting with his seat belt, then wishes us both a good day.

I get back inside, start the Mercedes. It is only then that I realize I have no idea where we are going. "Your destination?"

He looks at me for a moment, acknowledges the

cheekiness in my voice with a raised eyebrow. "Name a respectable Realtor," he says.

I blink, showing my confusion. "Realtor?"

"There's an agency off North Main, isn't there?"

"Yes," I say, "but the better one's just outside of town. Morgan's."

"You can drop me there then."

Now that I've had a moment, I do an admirable job of blanking my face of curiosity and not questioning his destination. We're there in ten minutes of talk-free driving, pulling into the small lot where I park beside a black Range Rover.

"Thanks for the ride," Tate says, looking at me.

"Do you want me to wait?" I ask.

"No," he says. "I'll get a taxi back to the hotel."

"They're not that easy to come by around here."

"Yeah. I'll ask someone for a ride."

I nod, as if this is fine with me. Which it is, of course. Why shouldn't it be? "Ask for Ann Morgan, if you want to see an agent."

"Okay," he says. "I will."

He tries to open the car door, and we realize, at the same time, he's going to need some help. I get out and go around, open it for him. He steps onto the pavement, looking more than a little bothered by his ineptitude.

"Thanks," he says. "For everything."

"You're welcome," I say, wondering if this is goodbye then.

He gives me a long look, and I take a step back, not sure what to do with it. A too-lengthy pause hangs between us, and then I say, "Okay. Take care."

I walk back to the driver's side, slide in, and close the

door. I start the car, swallow hard. I look up to find him standing in front of the hood.

"Wait," he says.

I lower the window. He walks around. "I thought I'd look for a place," he says.

"A place?" I repeat.

"To live. For a while."

"Oh." No explanation for the sudden tripping of my heart. "Here?"

"Here. I could use an expert local opinion," he says.

"Ann is very good," I say, trying to recover my equilibrium.

"From you," he says.

"From me?"

"If you have time."

"I'm not sure it's a good idea," I say, certain I am right.

"Probably not. But there aren't any strings attached."

"Oh. Well. Then." I have no idea what to make of this, and so I get out, lead the way inside.

Ann Morgan is talking to the receptionist at the front desk when we walk into the waiting area. She's a single mom with a daughter in Corey's class. We're both room mothers for class parties and such.

"Jillie," she says, spotting me. "Hey! What are you doing here?"

I step aside and wave a hand in Tate's direction. "Brought you a client," I say.

She redirects her gaze to Tate, her green eyes instantly lighting up with appreciation. "Have you now?"

"Tate Callahan," he says, lifting both hands in the air. "I'd shake, but—"

"But," she says. Ann grew up in South Carolina, and

her accent is soft and rounded at the edges. "Goodness gracious. What happened to you?"

"It's not as bad as it looks," he says.

"Good thing," Ann says, touching a hand to my shoulder, perceptive enough not to ask more. "What can I help you two with?"

She says "you two" with a question in her voice, and I know she is wondering whether he's mine or if he's fair game. "Tate is looking for a place to live."

Ann aims her laser-whitened smile at him. "Rent or buy?"

"Depends on the place," he says.

"Wait a minute." Ann puts a finger under her chin, stares hard at him.

"You're the writer! I can't believe I didn't recognize you. I just saw your picture somewhere—" She stops, visibly searching her memory. "Oh, and did you know we have another writer here at the lake? Bowie Dare. He married Keegan Monroe. You know them, don't you, Jillie?"

"Yes, we've met," I say.

"I'm sure you two would have lots in common," Ann redirects to Tate.

His voice is polite when he says, "Do you have anything you could show me?"

"I certainly do," Ann says, popping into gear as if aware she has again approached a line it would be better not to cross. "Can you look now?"

"Yes," he says. "Jillie?"

"Sure," I say. "Now is good."

23

Jillie

ANN DRIVES US all over the county, the diesel engine of her Mercedes so loud that we have to raise our voices to be heard above it.

Tate is in front, and I'm in the back, after insisting I will ride there. It's an interesting vantage point from which to watch Ann's increasingly flirtatious banter with this man who is the odd combination of the known and unknown to me. I can almost predict his response to her promptings, and it is a little shocking to realize I am still that tuned in to him.

We've hit hour number three of our Smith Mountain Lake real estate tour, when Ann pulls into a slot at Pinkins, one of the few drive-ins left in the region. This one has been around since 1954, still serves hot dogs, French fries, and frozen lemonade, irreverent of anything so impractical as cholesterol and triglycerides. The owner, Darryl Pinkins, likes to tout to naysayers that he's been eating the food for more than fifty years, and he's still here. I suppose he has a point.

A teenage waitress in pigtails comes out to ask what we'd like. We each order a lemonade, then sit sipping it while Ann flips through the MLS house listings, and I try not to think about the times Tate and I sat in this same parking lot in my dad's old Chevrolet truck, talking about our future. I wonder if he remembers.

"I think I've shown you just about everything that seems suitable for a single guy," Ann says, emphasis on single. She's starting to sound a little doubtful of her ability to find what he's looking for. But then, in all fairness, I don't think he's actually said what that is. I'm wondering myself.

The chunky book of listings sits on the console between them. Ann flips through it with her right hand, straw between her red-lipsticked lips.

"And you really didn't care for the Pacer place on Harbor Road?"

"I'd like a little more space around the house," he says.

"Um," she murmurs, still flipping pages. She stops at one, pokes a finger at a photo. "Well, here's something with space. What about the old Mason place?"

Tate leans over, studies the picture. She's talking about Cross Country, of course. I sit back, wait for Tate to nix it. I can tell by Ann's expression, she's expecting the same. Only he surprises us both. He asks about the price. She tells him, the number tossed out in a pretty-ridiculous-huh tone of voice.

"Let's take a look," he says.

Ann sits wide-eyed for a moment, not quite managing to hide her amazement. "Oh. Well. Absolutely," she says in the suddenly neutral tone of a good salesperson. She plops her lemonade in a cup holder, starts the car, and we make record time out of town, as if she's afraid he'll come to his senses and change his mind.

The whole way, Ann sings the praises of the old place, not realizing that we both already know everything there is to know about Cross Country.

And then some.

24

Tate

IT'S OBVIOUS THAT no one has lived at Cross Country for a good while.

The Realtor navigates the potholes of the farm's long driveway with a disapproving frown, her hands tight on the steering wheel, as if bracing for an oncoming wave.

I find it hard to believe the farm has sunk into its current state of neglect. As we approach the house, I notice how the rose bushes out front have grown into one another. There's at least a week's worth of weedeating to do along the visible fence lines alone. The pastures are a mass of overgrown grass and weeds.

Ann stops the car, and the three of us get out. I meet eyes with Jillie, instantly understanding the wounded pride I see in hers. I feel the need to defend the place in the same way I sense that she does, this old matriarch to whom we had once been so attached.

"Well," Ann says, clapping her hands together. "Let's take a look, shall we?" She leads the way up the steps and unlocks the front door. We walk inside the foyer, and I remember what a grand place it had once been. A curved staircase to our right leads to the upstairs of the house.

The original mirrors lining the staircase wall are still there, as if the idea of moving them had been too much to take on. An inch of dust cakes the windowsills and baseboards. A few pieces of furniture have been left along with the mirrors. They are covered with white sheets.

From the foyer, we walk into the enormous living room the Masons had so often used for entertaining. I had seen it only once or twice in the years when I'd tagged along after Jillie all over this place. At one end is a fieldstone fireplace wide enough to park a lawn tractor in. The windows at the front of the room are tall and wide, the glass panes wavy and thick. The floors are dark cherry, aged to a patina.

"It is awfully large for one person," Ann says, giving me a skeptical look.

"Would you mind waiting here while Jillie and I look at the rest?" I ask.

The question throws her, but I suspect she prides herself on being a professional because her expression is neutral when she says, "Of course. I have some e-mails to check on, anyway. You two make yourselves at home."

I lead the way to the kitchen, Jillie following behind me. I can feel her disbelief but choose to ignore it for now, taking in the extent of repair work that might be needed room to room. When we reach the staircase again, I step aside to let Jillie go up first. I had never been up to this part of the house when we were kids, but I know that she had. She leads me to the master bedroom, opens the heavy, wood door with its antique doorknob. A very wide-paned window makes up most of the back wall, providing a view of the horse barn and fields beyond.

"It's an incredible view," Jillie says, folding her arms across her chest.

"It is," I agree.

We're both silent for a bit. I can't help but wonder if she's remembering the times we found places to make out in those fields. If she's remembered over the years how we couldn't get enough of each other, how we lived for the next meeting, the next chance to be alone.

I'm remembering.

"You can't think this is a good idea, Tate," she says in a soft voice.

"Probably not," I say.

"Then why would you . . . why are you considering it?"

I look at her then, and it takes a second, but she finally turns her eyes to mine, as if she has no ability to stop herself. "Something about loose ends," I say.

It's clear that she wants to argue the wisdom of this. But she doesn't.

And I wonder if she understands that even though this place had never been my home, it had been the center of the only good memories I can claim from my teenage years. That I'm overcome with a sense of hitting solid ground after an entire adult life of drifting wherever the current happens to take me.

"You see it the way I see it, don't you?" I ask.

"What do you mean?"

"This place. Not as it is. But as it was. What it can still be."

She bites her lower lip, glances down at the floor, her gaze reluctantly pulling back to mine. "Yes," she says softly.

"That's all I needed to hear," I say.

25

Jillie

I HAVE TO pick up the girls, and so Ann drops me off at the real estate office. She's offered to take Tate to his hotel, and I get out of the car, stand for a moment next to Ann's rolled-down window, not sure what to say about what happened today. I still can't quite believe it. Have no idea what to make of it.

Tate thanks me for my help, polite as any stranger. I say sure, no problem, and wave as they pull away, as if this is something we do every day. In reality, I still haven't absorbed the absolute improbability of it all.

The girls are waiting out front when I pull up at the school, late enough that the other cars have come and gone.

"Where've you been?" Kala asks when she slides into the front seat, irritation rimming the words. This is a new thing with us, Kala's frequent unhappiness with me, and I have to say, it never fails to put a bruise on my heart.

"Helping an old friend," I say.

"Who is it?" Corey asks, plopping into the back, the rubber band from one of her pigtails barely holding on.

"No one you know," I say. Kala pops in ear buds, tuning me out. Corey tells me about her day, how Gerald Collins brought one of his dad's magazines to school and got in all sorts of trouble because none of the women inside had clothes on.

Driving the familiar roads to a place I have never been able to think of as home, I think about Tate and what he has done. I have no explanation for any of it, but something about it makes sense. He once loved that place every bit as much as I did.

I still can't believe that after all these years, he's actually here at Smith Mountain Lake. I've tried to picture him in other places, wondered where he lived, what his life was like. None of the images ever clicked because I simply couldn't imagine him anywhere else.

The thought of him at Cross Country is like finding the last, but most critical piece in a gigantic puzzle that is finally complete. And even if I never see Tate again, there's something immensely satisfying in knowing that he'll be there at Cross Country. Where both of us had once been happy.

26

Angela

SHE'S IN THE dry cleaner's shop, picking up two of her mother's dresses when news of Tate's purchase reaches her ears. Lu Styers makes change for a twenty, counts it out in Angela's hand while doing double duty in a phone conversation with her daughter.

"That writer bought the Mason place," she says, her voice going a couple of octaves higher. "Callahan, isn't it?"

Until now, Angela has been in a hurry, waiting a little too impatiently while Mrs. Styers retrieved the dresses from the rack in the back. But she takes her time now, tucking the money into her wallet, lifting the plastic bag from its hanger, hoping the older woman will drop a few more nuggets of gossip.

"Maybe he'll do something good with it," Mrs. Styers says. "From the road, you can barely see it anymore, it's so grown up with weeds."

The store owner glances up, and by now, it is obvious that Angela is lingering. She takes the dry cleaning and quickly leaves, shock rippling across her skin. She hits the remote to her BMW convertible, gets in, and sits behind the wheel, unmoving.

Tate. Had he actually bought the Mason farm?

She opens her purse, pulls the tabloid article from the side pocket, opens it and stares at the picture, then rereads the words, as she has done a dozen times in the past couple of days.

Angela drops her head against the back of the seat. Almost twenty years, and she had begun to think that piece of her life was one she would never have to revisit. That her own transgressions could be locked away, forgotten.

She presses her hands to the sides of her face, feeling as if the walls are closing in. She'd been so stupid.

Tate is back. And she finally admits to herself something she cannot deny.

She had known all along there would be a consequence for her actions.

After all, you cannot blow a hole in the center of someone's life and expect to never pay a price for it.

27

Tate

AT EIGHT O'CLOCK that evening, I get out of Ann's Mercedes in the circular driveway of the house at Cross Country.

She jangles a set of keys in the air. "I have to say I've never had a transaction quite like this one. Who says cash doesn't talk? Done deal in a day."

"Thanks for going the extra mile," I say.

She waves a hand. "Are you kidding? I'm real estate royalty in my agency for selling this place. I should be thanking you."

I follow her up the stone steps, past the overgrown azaleas to the massive, walnut door at the house's entrance. She inserts a key in the lock, and it swings open. "Let me get your things out of the trunk," she says. "You go on in. I'll be right back."

I start to protest, but then glance at my hands and realize I have little choice but to accept her help. The cumbersome bandages are beginning to get old already.

I walk through the two-story foyer, flicking on lights with my elbow as I go. Dust sits thick on the stairway's heavy banister. Cobwebs hang between the rails.

To my left is the enormous living room, which I had seen only once or twice in the years when I'd tagged along after Jillie all over this place.

The door opens again, and Ann clicks inside on her high heels. She sets my laptop bag and overnight duffel outside the living room doorway, then comes into the room.

"Incredible, isn't it?"

"It's a beautiful house," I say.

"I can't wait to see what you do with it," she says. "It's a crying shame to let a place like this go to ruin. Do you have anything in mind?"

The question incites in me a sudden urge to laugh. If I'd been asked just yesterday about the chances of me buying a house on Smith Mountain Lake, I'd have said less than zero. And yet, here I stand in the middle of this mausoleum of a home, with no idea what I plan to do with it.

Nothing to attach me to it at all except a bunch of memories long past their expiration date. "Not exactly," I say.

"Well, if you should need any help, I know a great interior designer. And I've been told I have a decent eye for renovation."

"Thanks," I say, hearing the undernote of something else in her voice.

She's an attractive woman, and more than once throughout the day, I've felt her interest. I wonder if Jillie had noticed, and then tell myself it hardly matters one way or the other.

"I appreciate everything, Ann."

"Well," she says. "Let me just get your pillows and blankets out of the car, and I'll be off."

I meet her at the front door a minute later. She offers to carry my stuff upstairs, but I tell her I'll manage.

"Sleep well, then," she says.

I stand at the door until she pulls away and heads back down the winding driveway to the main road. Once she's out of sight, I close the door, standing in the middle of the grand foyer that had once seemed to me like the entrance to another life entirely. I'm overcome with the oddest sense of past and present merging. And a single question. What have I done?

That One Night

THE PARTIES AT Cross Country were known to outclass anything else ever held in the county. Sonya Mason never did anything on a small scale.

The event this Saturday night was no exception. It marked the celebration of her biggest win to date in the jumping world. Just the day before, she had returned from the show at Madison Square Garden in New York City where four of the Cross Country horses had won pretty much everything there was to win.

Tate still felt as if the entire previous week was something from which he would most certainly wake to discover as a dream. People like him didn't get to experience the things they'd seen and done at the show.

When they weren't working or riding, he and Jillie covered every inch of Manhattan they could possibly manage on foot.

The thought of the city had never appealed to him

before. In fact, he'd all but dreaded going, sure it would remind him too much of his earlier childhood in the poorest area of D.C. But seeing the city with Jillie made it different. He didn't see the dirt on the sidewalks. Noticed, instead, how blue the sky was between the rows of enormous buildings. And that pretty much defined everything about what he felt for her.

He stood at the foot of the winding staircase of the main house now, hands shoved in the pockets of the suit he'd borrowed from Jillie's dad. The shoulders were a little too wide, and the waist of the pants hung loose, even with his belt in the last notch. He felt awkward and out of place, but Jillie wanted him here, and for that reason alone, he could endure the suit.

Dr. Mason spotted Tate and walked over, clapping him on the shoulder.

"They'll be down in a few minutes, son. All that primping takes time."

"Yes, sir," Tate said. Mrs. Mason was giving Jillie the special treatment tonight as a thank you for her winning ride at the National Horse Show in Madison Square Gardens. He wasn't sure exactly what that involved, but they'd been up there for a long time.

Just then Mrs. Mason and Jillie appeared at the top of the stairs. Both Tate and Dr. Mason went silent and stared.

"There," the older man said. "You see. They take forever, but they are worth the wait, aren't they?"

Tate nodded, unable to find his voice. Jillie walked down, one slow step at a time, careful in the high heels she wasn't used to wearing. At the bottom of the staircase, she looked down at her dress, as if she weren't sure what his reaction would be.

Sonya Mason smiled and said, "This is the part where you say how beautiful she looks, Tate."

"I—" he began, and then, "Wow."

Mrs. Mason laughed. "Jillie, I don't think we can ask for more than that."

Dr. Mason chuckled, took his wife's hand and said, "You're a knockout yourself, and you owe me a dance."

The two of them headed for the terrace at the back of the house where a band was playing classics, like "Fly Me to the Moon."

Tate found himself unable to look directly at Jillie, because every time he did, he lost all train of thought. She touched his shoulder. "Dance?"

"Yeah," he said, following her to the back of the house where they stepped into the middle of the dancing throng of people. For a while, they danced apart, but then the music slowed, couples drifting into each other's arms.

He and Jillie had never danced this way before, and he suddenly felt awkward and unsure of himself. But no sooner had she stepped up close to him than his arms went around her waist, and it felt like the most natural thing in the world that they should be together like this.

They danced in a small circle, bodies pressed close, eyes only for each other. Tate couldn't bring himself to stop looking at her. Her long, blonde hair was pulled back in a loose clip, her neck long and graceful in the V-cut, black dress.

Looking at her, Tate felt as if he were the luckiest guy in the world. Once the music changed, Jillie linked her hand with his, pulled him across the terrace and through the backyard where the lights were dim.

They stopped beside a short, rock wall that served as a divider between the grass lawn and a hay field. They stood side by side, shoulders touching. He still couldn't look at her.

She touched a hand to his arm. "It's just a dress. It's still me, Tate."

He did look at her then, found her studying him with warm, appreciative eyes. "I know," he said. "You're just . . . you're beautiful, Jillie."

"Thank you," she said. "Coming from you, it means something."

She leaned in then and kissed him. And it was like a thousand rockets going off above them, what he felt inside. He pulled her close against him, deepened the kiss. Her arms went around his neck, and they stayed that way for a long time, while the music from the house drifted out and fell around them.

"Oops, didn't realize this was the make-out site!" A giggle followed the exclamation.

Tate and Jillie stepped away from each other. He turned to find Angela Taylor and Poppy Sullivan arm in arm, their ability to stay vertical apparently impaired by the glasses of champagne in their hands.

He stepped in front of Jillie, shielding her while she adjusted her clothes.

"Is this what happens when you have a big win, Jillie?" Poppy's voice was sloppy drunk. "You get the trophy and the guy?"

Angela laughed, and then cut it short when she met Tate's unamused gaze.

Jillie stepped out from behind him.

"Whoa!" Poppy said. "And a makeover too."

Angela backed up a step and said, "Come on, Poppy."

"Why?" the other girl said. "This is obviously where all the fun is."

"I think you better listen to Angela," Tate said.

Poppy made a face, staggered a step, splashing champagne down the front of her dress. "As if she knows how to have fun?" She waved a hand in dismissal. She looked at Jillie, then teetered forward and placed her hand on Tate's chest. She put her mouth close to his ear, whispered, "Come with me, and we can really get this party started."

He put his hands on her shoulders, forced her to move back. "Poppy. Go."

She pointed a finger at Jillie. "What on earth has that tomboy got that could possibly interest you? Aren't you the kind of guy who needs the real thing? Not some little girl pretending to be a grown-up?"

"You don't have any idea what kind of guy he is, Poppy," Jillie said, stepping up to stand between Tate and the other girl.

Poppy's laugh was harsh at the edges. "Oh, I think I do," she said. "He's no different from the rest. One thing is what they're all interested in. And don't tell me you would have any idea how to give it to him."

"Poppy—" Angela pulled at her arm, sounding suddenly more sober.

"Come on. Let's go."

Poppy jerked her arm away. "That's just like you, Ang. You've had a crush on him for how many years now? And instead of taking the matter head on, you just stand back and moon over why someone like Jillie has beaten you out."

Tate glanced at Angela, saw the way her face crumpled beneath the words. She turned and ran back across the yard.

"Angela!" Tate called after her, but she kept going.

Poppy laughed. "Why don't you go get her, Tate? I'm sure consolation from you would just make it all better."

Jillie stepped forward, shoved the girl backwards. Poppy landed hard on her backside, her dress ending up around her waist.

"What is wrong with you?" Jillie screamed.

Poppy looked down at her now-ruined dress, held her hands up as if she couldn't believe what Jillie had just done. She finally got to her feet, gave Jillie a long, cold glare. "One day, you're going to pay for that," she said, and walked off.

"She's a preacher's daughter," Tate said after a few moments. "What the heck?"

They sat down on the rock wall, a chunk of space between them now.

"Maybe I should go find her," Jillie said.

"Angela?"

"Yeah. I suspect she's pretty humiliated."

He turned his head, looked at her for a long moment. "She might not take it so well from you."

"Maybe not. But then there is something the two of us have in common."

"What's that?" he said.

"We both figured out early on that you were something special."

He glanced away, wondered if she had any idea just how devoid his life had been of such statements. Sometimes, he couldn't quite believe that Jillie could really feel anything for him. He looked at her then, leaned over and kissed her, this time holding nothing back.

Everything he felt for her was right there. Laid out as honestly as he could put it. When he finally pulled away, she smiled at him and said, "Me too."

She got up then, walked across the dimly lit yard, stopping a short distance away to turn once and look at him again. They didn't say anything. They didn't need to.

28

Jillie

I SPEND THE next few days in a state of high alert. Other than a call from Ann thanking me profusely for sending her Tate as a client, I've heard nothing more of his move to Cross Country. I'm not sure what it is I'm expecting, but it seems something short of anticlimactic for him to be in such close proximity for the first time in so many years and not see him. But then, what else do I imagine might be in store for us?

We don't really even know each other anymore. Whatever we'd once had is long gone, and I know nothing about his life now.

And so I try not to think about him, to go back to that point just a week ago when I lived with the acceptance that I would never see him again. It's easier that way. Wiser, without doubt.

I put my concentration on my daughters, on being a good mother. With Corey, it is easy. With Kala, it is not.

If anything, she has become more distant, avoids me

even. I try to talk to her about it, and she closes me out, unwilling to discuss what is bothering her. I try to remember the things I felt at her age. But it feels as though it's more than teenage angst. Deeper. Blacker.

On Thursday night, I've just finished helping Corey with her homework. Spelling again, and she's getting better at it. She's just spelled Mississippi without missing a letter.

"I think that deserves an ice cream cone," I say, closing the book. We're in the backyard at the picnic table. Dusk has started to settle. "Why don't you run up and ask Kala if she wants to go?"

Corey bounds off across the grass with a yip. Ice cream is at the top of her list of favorite things.

I get my purse and keys and head for the front door. Corey meets me at the bottom of the stairs, a little of the pleasure gone from her face. "Kala doesn't want to go," she says.

"Oh," I say. "Did she say why?"

Corey shrugs. "Just doesn't want to."

I consider going up and getting her, but decide to let it go. Corey and I drive to the Dairy Queen where she orders a double vanilla scoop dipped in chocolate. I splurge and order the same. Corey finishes hers before we get back home. I eat half of mine and throw the rest away, deeply worried about Kala's increasing distance.

Upstairs, I walk Corey to her room. "Time for bed, honey," I say. "Go brush your teeth."

"Okay. Thanks for the ice cream, Mama," she says, kissing me on the cheek and then skating across the wood floor to the bathroom in her socks.

Kala is sitting on her bed, a book propped up on her knees. "Wish you'd gone with us," I say.

She lifts a shoulder, doesn't look up from the page.

I go over, sit down on the corner of the mattress. "Hey. Can we talk?"

She looks up then, doesn't answer.

"What's going on?" I ask.

"Nothing, Mom," she says in a voice that completely contradicts her answer.

I put my hand on her knee, squeeze once. "I can't help, if I don't know what it is."

She throws her legs over the other side of her bed, her back to me, stiff and unyielding. Kala has always been a child from whom I have to pull answers. She keeps things to herself until the wear of it is clear on her face. "I don't want to live here anymore," she says suddenly.

I feel my heart wrench with the pain beneath the words. I understand how she feels. I don't want to live here either. Nor do I want my two daughters to hate me when Judith poisons their minds with her version of what happened between Jeffrey and me.

I put my hand on her shoulder. "Kala. I'm sorry—"

She jerks around then, her face red with anger. "You're sorry! You're always sorry! Why can't you just do something to make it different?"

"Kala—"

She erupts from the bed, hands on her hips. "I mean what do you do here all day, anyway? Aren't you bored? Don't you want to do something with your life other than answer to Grandma twenty-four seven?"

Each word is like an arrow through the center of my chest. Painful for the simple reason that they are bathed in truth. And too, for the realization that in my daughter's eyes, I am a serious disappointment.

She's right though. I have no idea who I am anymore.

Any thread of the woman I had once hoped to be is so deeply woven into this existence I have managed to call a life that it is barely identifiable, even to me.

But how do I tell her the real answer? That I am trapped in a prison of my own making.

29

Kala

SHE HAS NEVER once spoken to her mother this way. Remorse seeps up like water filling her lungs, making her feel as if she can't breathe.

Through the dark, she runs from the house to the barn, tripping once and nearly falling. She lets herself in one of the side doors, climbs the ladder to the hayloft where she sits above the top rung, peering down at the horses in their stalls. She's woken them, but a minute later, they're resuming their sleeping stance, one hind foot propped behind them, heads lowered.

She'd been so mean. Knows she hurt her mom just now. But it's as if she can't help it. She's just so angry. And it's like this huge red tarp of fury covers everything she tries to do. No matter how hard she forces it back down inside her, it won't stay, and it's scary how it's starting to take control of her.

She props her elbows on her knees, runs both hands

through her hair. She should go back and say she's sorry. But she's not sure she can.

Because she really doesn't want to live here anymore. And really does wonder how her mom can keep being her grandmother's doormat. Available to wipe her feet on whenever she wants to.

She's supposed to love her grandma. She knows that. But sometimes, people just make it impossible to love them. How many insults should a person swallow and accept as truth before there's not a speck of space inside them for more?

This afternoon had been a perfect example. Kala had been working on her homework at the kitchen table when her grandmother walked in and made herself a cup of hot tea without saying a word. Once she'd poured a cup, she stood by the sink, studying Kala, her disapproving gaze settling on the three chocolate chip cookies lined up beside her notebook.

"You aren't eating all of those, are you, dear?"

Kala glanced at the cookies, warmth flooding her face. "I didn't have much lunch."

Her grandmother made a clucking noise. "Girls who eat like that are destined to be fat. Haven't we taught you better food choices?"

Kala's gaze stayed on the page of the book she'd been reading, the words a blur. "Yes, ma'am."

Her grandmother picked up the cookies, dropped them in the sink disposal. "Fat thighs are hardly attractive on a rider." She opened the refrigerator door, pulled out a mini bag of carrots and put them in front of Kala. "A much better choice."

Kala's cheeks burn now with the replaying of the

scene. It is not the first, however. And she knows it will not be the last.

Her mother endures the same kind of constant putdowns. Kala cannot begin to understand why.

She knows the story about her mother's life before she got married. How she was this big-time, junior rider, made a name for herself on the jumper show circuit, until one day she just walked away and never went back. Or at least this was what her dad told her. Only she's beginning to wonder if there is more to the story. She doesn't see how someone could have a gift like that and just throw it away. Never look at it again.

Cricket, Corey's pony, sneezes. Munchy, Kala's gelding in the stall beside Corey, takes a long draw from the automatic waterer. It clicks on and refills, and then the barn is silent again.

More than anything, Kala wants to leave Stone Meadow. She's thought about all the scary stuff. Will they have to leave their horses here?

Where would they live? How would her mother be able to afford to take care of them?

She has no answers for any of the questions. She only knows she has to go. Whether her mom and Corey do or not. She has to go.

30

Tate

SO HERE I AM.

Smack dab in the middle of a life I had once dreamed of having. And I have no idea what to do with it.

I've spent the past few days making the house livable. Buying some furniture for the living room. Table and chairs for the kitchen. King-size bed in the upstairs, master bedroom. All this, and still, it is a house that feels empty.

I grab a bottle of water from the refrigerator, go out back to the porch that looks across a pasture where thoroughbreds had once grazed. It's empty too and something about this feels so wrong.

This place had once teemed with life and purpose. It is devoid now of anything remotely resembling that.

I sit in a rickety rocker and stare into the dark, flexing my left hand, grimacing a little at its stiffness. I'd paid a couple of guys from the hotel where I had been staying to drive my car over a couple of days ago. I managed to drive myself to the hospital yesterday, where a doctor had removed the bandages from my hands. Both are still sore, but I'm grateful to be able to use them again.

My thoughts turn to Jillie, as they have countless times these past few days. I've tried not to think about her, telling myself they have nowhere to go. Bitterness still sits like a rock in my chest, and I cannot imagine ever putting our past behind us. Some things are just too big, too painful to ever get beyond.

I hear a noise in the yard, peer out through the dark, but don't see anything. Probably a deer. They graze in the yard at night, a herd of six or seven. I've spotted them at dawn when I get up.

I sit back in the chair, taking a sip of water. There's the noise again. I stand this time, go outside, and walk into the yard. The light from the house allows for some visibility, and I think I spot something a few feet away. A soft whine, barely audible, lifts out of the darkness.

I go inside and get a flashlight, then come back out, throwing the beam across the backyard. Sitting in the grass is a little tan and white Beagle. Hunched forward and shaking. No collar. A bundle of skin and bones.

"Hey," I say.

The dog scoots back a few feet, continuing to shake.

It's warm outside, so I can only assume it's scared to death. I drop down on my knee, lower my voice. "You want something to eat?"

The dog whimpers.

"Let me see what I can find," I say, getting up and going back into the house.

I return a minute later with a can of chicken, from which I awkwardly manage to pull the lid. It comes off with a little pop that sends the dog scuttling back to a safer distance. I dump the chicken in a bowl, then drop down onto my knees and set it in the grass. The dog eyes it for several moments, then creeps forward, as if there are mines beneath its feet. On shaking legs, it gulps the chicken, as if it hasn't had food in days.

As soon as the bowl is empty, the dog retreats in a whipflash to its former stance, sits and stares at me, still shaking.

"That took a lot of courage, didn't it?"

The dog whimpers again.

I pick up the bowl, carry it over to the water spigot, rinse it out, then fill it and set it just below the porch step.

But this time, the dog stays where it is, apparently unconvinced the water is worth the risk. I wait for a good while, coaxing it forward without success. I finally give up. "All right. I'll leave it there."

I go inside the house, turning at the door of the screened porch to look back at the dog once more.

It's still sitting there, watching me.

It occurs to me then that I have never in my life owned a dog, cat, or anything else requiring commitment. I could argue that I've never been in a position to care for anything other than myself. But then that's not exactly true. The truth is I've lived a life free of such entanglements, because part of me believes attachments only lead to hurt.

I no longer remember exactly how many foster homes I lived in before I was finally placed with the Templetons here at the lake. But I do remember how with the first few, I had let myself start to think it might be permanent. Start to care about the people I lived with, their dogs and cats too. And always, I had to leave them behind. Each time, I left a chunk of my heart with them.

The last and final lesson had been Jillie. With Jillie, I'd torn down all the walls, made myself vulnerable in a way I never had before. I'd loved my life here. Leaving it, leaving her, had nearly killed me.

I leave the porch light on and go upstairs, wondering if the dog will still be there in the morning. Probably not. And, anyway, I should know that's for the best.

31

Kala

SHE WATCHES FROM the pitch-dark edge of the yard, hunched down beside an enormous boxwood.

The little dog, a Beagle, maybe, sits for a long time after the man goes in, then finally darts over to the bowl and laps the water, as if it can't get it in fast enough.

Kala waits until she sees the light flick off behind the drawn shade of the upstairs window. No one had lived here in years, and she is disappointed to see that the house is no longer empty.

A few hours ago, she'd climbed into her bed with her clothes still on beneath her nightgown, pretending to be asleep when her mother came in to check on her.

When the house was quiet, she tiptoed around her room, throwing a few things into her bag and leaving a sleeping Corey in the bed beside hers. That part had been hard, but slipping out the back door of the big house at Stone Meadow, Kala felt a lifting of something she couldn't even explain to herself.

She ran down the long driveway and out to the main road, where she'd walked the five miles to Cross Country, intending to spend the night in the little, white house where her mother had grown up, even if she had to break a window to get in.

She darts across the yard now, staying in the shadows, her backpack jostling on her shoulder. The grass beneath her shoes is wet with dew, and she's afraid to turn on the small flashlight in her hand for fear the man will see her. She finds the board fence line and follows it to the horse barn, then darts across a paved parking lot bordering the little house.

She hears a noise behind her, looks back to see that the little dog is following her. It stays at a distance, stops when she stops. "You have to be quiet," she whispers.

At the house, Kala goes around back, turning the flashlight on for a few moments to find her way. Three steps lead to a door. She turns the knob. It's locked. She stands for a moment, thinking.

The door has a row of panes just above the knob. Would it be so wrong to break one? She could send money to pay for it later.

Right now, she's so tired, and if she can just sleep for a little while, she'll be able to figure out where she'll go in the morning. She takes the butt of the flashlight and jabs it against the glass. It shatters, the sound so loud that she is sure it will wake the man in the big house.

The dog barks from its viewing spot several yards away.

"Shh," Kala says again, terrified now. She could go to jail if she's caught. She looks up at the big house, waits to see if the upstairs light flicks on. When it remains dark, she breathes a sigh of relief and opens the door.

She turns to look back at the dog who is still watching her.

"You can come in if you want," she says.

The dog whines, lies down on the grass with its head on its paws.

"Okay, then," she says. "You'll let me know if anyone comes?"

Another whine is the reply, and she can only hope that's a yes.

32

Tate

I AWAKE THE next morning to a slat of sunlight slipping through the window blinds. It's not quite six. I get up, take a shower, then go downstairs and make some coffee.

I take the cup outside, disappointed to see that the dog is not there. But then I hadn't really expected it to be.

I sit down on the porch step, sip my coffee and wonder how I will fill the hours of the day stretched out before me. The book is going nowhere, and I'm sick of sitting in front of my blinking computer screen, as if waiting for some sort of divine inspiration to strike.

I glance at the barn and then the house that sits at the corner of the driveway a short distance from it.

Something at the back catches my attention, and I lean to the left for a better look. Recognizing the Beagle, I put down my coffee cup and walk that way.

At the sight of me, the dog hunkers down and rolls

over, as if it is sure the sky is about to fall, and I am the cause of it.

Realizing he's a boy, I squat a few feet away and hold out my hand. "You did hang around, didn't you, fella?"

He rolls back over, studies me with big brown eyes, a soft whine coming from his throat.

"How about some more of that chicken?" I get up and turn toward the main house. He lets out another whine and glances at the guest house.

It's then that I notice the broken pane on the door.

I don't remember it being like that when I checked things out before.

I walk over, turn the knob, and find it unlocked. I open the door and stick my head inside. More broken glass on the floor. Whoever did it is probably long gone by now. I decide to take a look around anyway.

The kitchen is small, but I remember the countless dinners I'd had here with Jillie and her father. This house had felt more like a home to me than any I'd ever lived in.

I walk down a narrow hall to the living room, coming to an abrupt stop when I spot a young girl curled up by the fireplace, her head resting on a navy backpack.

As if sensing my presence, she comes awake with a jolt, sitting straight up and squinting at me. "Oh, my gosh," she says.

I'm a little stunned by the words, the voice, the face. She's no more than fifteen years old, and it is as if I've been bolted back in time.

"Who are you?" I ask, somehow already knowing the answer.

She scrambles to her feet, slips the backpack over her shoulders. "I'm sorry. I'll go. I know I shouldn't have broken the door, but I just needed a place to sleep—"

She edges the room, slips past me, and heads for the back door. "I'm sorry. I won't be back again."

I follow her outside, reaching for her arm to stop her. "Whoa, whoa. Not so fast."

The Beagle, sitting a few yards away, barks once. The girl glances at it. Her face brightens for a moment.

"Is that your dog?" I ask.

"No," she says. "I saw you feeding him last night."

I study her for a moment, not sure what to do. Obviously, she's running from something. And not old enough to be doing so by herself. "He looks like he could use some more food. Come on up to the house, and I'll fix you both some breakfast."

She takes a step back, raises a hand. "Thanks, but I have to be going."

"Any place in particular?"

She shakes her head.

"You're Jillie's daughter, aren't you?"

Surprise flits across her face. "How do you know that?"

"You look almost exactly like her when she was your age."

"You knew her then?"

"I did. We were . . . really good friends."

She doesn't say anything for several moments, as if this is a little much for her to process.

"I make pretty good pancakes," I say.

She lifts a shoulder, considering.

Without waiting for her answer, I call the Beagle and head for the house.

33

Jillie

I LET THE GIRLS sleep until almost seven, even though we need to be out the door at seven-thirty. I'd had a restless night, too many thoughts to keep at bay long enough to allow sleep to take over.

I open the door of their room, stepping into the darkened interior. "Girls? Time to get up for school."

Corey is curled up in a ball, the covers thrown aside, as they always are at some point during the night. Kala's bed is empty. My heart knocks a little. I go to the bathroom door, find it open. She's not there.

"Corey?"

"Hmm?" she responds, still groggy.

"Where's Kala? Did she already go downstairs?"

"I don't know. Why?"

"Be right back," I say. Kala never gets up before she's called, but I go downstairs to look for her anyway. Lucille is in the kitchen, popping bread into the toaster. She looks up at me and says good morning.

"Good morning, Lucille. Have you seen Kala?"

"No," she answers, wiping her hands on her apron. "I got here at six. Haven't seen her."

"Thanks," I say and head down to the barn on the off chance that she's there.

Jess, the barn manager, is already there and feeding the horses their grain. I ask if she's seen Kala, somehow expecting her to say no, which she does.

I walk back to the house, forcing myself to remain calm. There is some explanation for this, something logical. But every awful story I have ever heard about children being taken from their beds in the middle of the night races through my mind, and I draw in a deep breath to force calm through my veins.

I have no idea what to do. Should I wait and see if she comes back? Where could she have gone? Is there a boy in her life, someone she hasn't told me about?

I consider whether I should call the police, but the very thought is like a rock in my stomach. Because that's like admitting that something bad has happened. And I can't do that. Not yet.

I grab my cell phone from my room and return to the edge of Corey's bed. She stretches hard, opens her eyes, and says, "What are you doing, Mama?"

"Kala's not here, honey," I say. "Can you think of anything she said that might help us know where to look for her."

Corey fiddles with the edge of her sheet. "Grandma made a big deal about her eating cookies after school yesterday."

I study my youngest daughter with a growing knot of anger inside me. "Did Kala tell you that?"

She shakes her head. "I heard it."

"Did she say anything to you?"

"No. She never does. Only to Kala. Kala asked me if I think she's fat."

I press my lips together, fury a sudden red haze before my eyes. How could a grandmother be so cruel? But with the anger, I feel a weighting sense of guilt for the fact that I have allowed my daughter to be subjected to this. I pray nothing horrible has happened to her. I pray for a chance to right this.

I have to find her. I turn the phone over, start to dial 911 and report my daughter missing. Before I finish punching in the numbers, the phone rings. I click the talk button, panic in my voice. "Hello?"

"Jillie."

His is the last voice I expect to hear. For a moment, I cannot respond.

"Are you there?"

"Yes," I manage.

"Your daughter. She's here at my house."

"Your house?"

"Cross Country."

Relief swamps me in a wave. I drop back against the headboard of the bed, suddenly weak and tearful. "She's . . . why? I've been looking everywhere—"

"She's okay," he says, his voice calm, reassuring.

I start to cry then, mortified to be doing so in his ear, and at the same time, completely unable to stop.

"I offered to bring her home, but she says no. Do you want to come over?"

I have a hundred questions, and yet, right now, none of the answers matter. I just want to see my daughter. Put my arms around her and know that she is really okay. "I'll be right there," I say.

34

Kala

SHE CAN ONLY imagine how mad her mom is going to be. It doesn't happen very often. Her mom has always been willing to talk when she's done things wrong. But somehow, Kala knows this is going to be different. The knowledge taints the taste of the otherwise passable pancakes the man has made her.

They eat without talking. When they're finished, she helps him clean up the dishes, and then follows him out to the front porch where they sit on the steps and wait for her mom. The Beagle takes a spot on the grass below, next to a huge old boxwood. Head on his paws, he closes his eyes and sleeps.

"I don't even know your name," Kala says, when the silence becomes too uncomfortable.

"It's Tate. Tate Callahan."

She studies him for a moment, the name ringing familiar in her ears.

Recognition hits her then. "You're my mom's friend from when she was growing up."

He nods, looks off down the driveway. "I moved here when I was twelve to live with a foster family. Your mom kind of made me her project."

Kala frowns at his choice of words. From what little she's gleaned from her mother's remarks, they'd been best friends. "Did you ride with my mom here at Cross Country?"

"I helped with the horses, watched her make a name for herself."

Kala stares at the barn, the empty pastures. "Why did she quit riding?"

He looks at her hard, as if he's surprised by the question. Her whole life, she's felt as if there's some part of her mom she's never really known. As if she locked it up and refused to ever open the door again.

"I don't know," he answers in a quiet voice. "It's not something I would ever have imagined her doing."

"She was really good, huh?"

"Really good," he says.

"Good enough to go to the Olympics?"

"I never doubted that was where she'd end up. She was fearless."

Kala is quiet for several long moments, and then, "It's like you're talking about a different person. Someone I don't know."

He rubs a hand across the knee of his jeans, an expression on his face she can't quite read. "Sometimes we change when we grow up, stop wanting things we once wanted."

The sound of tires on gravel pulls their gazes to the end

of the long driveway. Kala's stomach does a little dip at the sight of her mom's vehicle.

She pulls to a stop at the end of the yard, cuts the engine and quickly gets out, walking toward them too fast and then checking her pace.

"Kala," she says a few yards away from the front porch.

"Hi, Mom," Kala says reluctantly.

"I'll let you two talk," Mr. Callahan says, standing and disappearing into the house.

Kala's mom walks over to the steps, sits down beside her. "I'm glad you're okay," she says.

"Sorry if I made you worry."

She doesn't say anything for several long seconds, and then, "Do you want to tell me what's going on?"

Kala shrugs. "What difference will it make?"

"A lot, actually."

"I don't belong there anymore."

"You belong there as much as any of us."

Kala meets her mother's gaze then and says what she's wanted to say for a long time. "Do we belong there, Mom?"

Her mom starts to answer, but stops, silent, as if carefully considering her words. "It was your father's home. He wanted you there."

"But he's not there anymore. He left us."

"Kala, your father's choice had nothing to do with you."

"I don't think Grandma sees it that way."

"Your grandmother is angry."

"I'm angry too. But I don't take it out on her."

"I know. It's not fair."

"Then why do we stay there?"

Kala's mother looks down at her hands, as if she's searching for an answer.

"What happened to all your dreams, Mom? Mr. Callahan says you wanted to go to the Olympics. You never told us that."

"I wanted a lot of things. But part of growing up is understanding what's real and what isn't."

"So growing up means letting go of your dreams?"

With her gaze on the little, white house near the barn, she says, "Yes, sometimes, it does."

Kala jumps up from the steps, suddenly more furious than she can ever remember being. "Only if you're a coward!" She takes off running then toward the barn and the little, white house where she'd spent the night. From beneath the lower branches of a huge old boxwood, the Beagle scoots out and follows her at a run.

At the little house, Kala opens the door and lets the dog in behind her, shutting out her mom and all her broken dreams.

35

Jillie

I SIT FOR several long seconds after Kala disappears into the house I had grown up in. It's strange to see her opening the door I'd opened so many times, going back and forth between there and the barn. I start to go after her, but stop myself from doing so. I don't know what to say to her, how to bridge the ever-increasing chasm between us.

The door behind me opens, and Tate steps out onto the porch.

"Everything okay?" he asks.

I want to say yes, of course, but I can't. I've never been good at pretending something is true when it isn't. And certainly not with him.

"No," I say.

He sits down next to me. A foot or more separates us, but we might as well be skin to skin. All the old electricity is still there. I force my gaze to the barn and instead think about how sad it is all closed up and empty.

"I know it's none of my business, but she seems pretty unhappy," Tate says.

"She is," I agree.

"Have the two of you talked about why?"

I nod. "Since Jeffrey died . . . it's been hard. Maybe she blames me somehow."

"That's a lot for any kid to process."

"I know. She doesn't want to live at Stone Meadow. Jeffrey's mother . . . she can be very critical."

"Of Kala?"

"Of the world," I say, and then wish that I hadn't. The slip reveals too much information, invites pity, and I don't want that from Tate.

"Why do you stay?" he asks, and now he's looking off in the direction of the barn too, as if he doesn't trust himself to meet eyes with me.

"That would involve a very long and complicated answer."

"I don't have anywhere to be."

I take the opportunity to divert the conversation. "Surely you do."

"For now, I don't."

I hesitate, then ask, "So what's the deal, Tate? Why did you really buy this place?"

He looks off at the green fields beyond the barn, shrugs. "Unfinished business?"

"What does that mean?" I ask, alarm pinging through me.

"Don't worry, Jillie. I'm not here for revenge."

We sit with that for a few moments. "Then, why?"

He takes a long time to answer. I just wait.

He doesn't look at me when he finally says, "It feels like maybe I'm at a point to stop and think about where I'm going next in life. This seemed like a good place to do that thinking."

"A run-down farm in a place you said you were never coming back to?"

"It's not the first time I've done something I said I'd never do again."

The words hang between us. Part of me wants him to go on. Part of me doesn't.

"Why don't you help me get it back in shape?"

The question drops out of the air between us. My eyes go wide. "What?"

"The farm. Help me bring it back to life as a horse farm, and we'll split the profit on the resale."

The idea is so preposterous that I can't think what to say. "Why would you do that?"

He doesn't answer for long enough that I'm convinced he's already changed his mind. But his voice is low and certain when he says, "Loose ends, I guess."

I want to ask him exactly what he means by that, but I'm not sure I really want to know the answer. "There's an old saying about not opening doors if you can't handle what's behind them."

"But if you never open the door, how do you know for sure what's behind it?"

"I think maybe it's safer not to know." I stand and put some deliberate space between us. "I have to go."

"Say you'll think about it."

"Thanks for calling me about Kala," I say, ignoring the request.

I walk down to the little house and open the front door, calling my daughter's name. To my surprise, she appears within seconds. "Let's go home," I say.

"We don't have a home," she says, stepping past me to walk to the car. The Beagle trots out behind her.

As I pull around the circular driveway, Kala raises her hand to Tate. He waves back. I glance in the rearview mirror as we drive away. The Beagle is now sitting on the step next to Tate.

Kala looks back and says, "Lucky dog."

I don't disagree.

36

Jillie

KALA AND I drive home in silence. I want to talk, but can feel the wall of resistance between us. So I remain silent, painful as it is to let the wounds fester.

It wasn't so long ago that I could feel Kala's love every time she looked at me.

Had I taken it for granted? I want to say no, of course not, but I think I did in the way we do with anything we value that hasn't been threatened. Kala had loved her daddy in the same way, and I can only imagine how a child her age reasons a father's deliberate choice to leave his life.

I want to talk about this with her, begin the complicated unraveling of the choking strands of Kala's grief. I want to. But I cannot push a single word past my lips. I don't know how.

As soon as we pull up to the house at Stone Meadow, Kala jumps out of the car and runs inside. Feeling a new weight on my shoulders, I want only to reach the solitude of my own room where I can try to make sense of what has happened this morning. Chart a path for moving forward.

But that isn't to be. Judith appears in the foyer just as I walk inside the door. The look of irritation on her face tells me she's been waiting for us.

"Why isn't Kala in school today?" she snaps.

It's impossible not to be offended by Judith's high-handed manner, but I force an even note to my voice when I say, "She's not feeling well."

"Lucille said you couldn't find her this morning."

"It was just a misunderstanding," I say.

"I will not have you lying to my face, Jillian," Judith says, arms crossed in righteous indignation.

It's certainly not the first time Judith has spoken to me this way. But I find myself unable to ignore it this morning. "As mother and daughter, we have a right to some amount of privacy. What is going on between Kala and me is none of your business."

Shock whitens her face. "Certainly, you don't think I'm going to accept your speaking to me in that tone of voice."

"Oh, I'm sorry. That's a one-way street, isn't it?"

"Jillian!"

I realize I have shocked her, and, to be honest, I'm not sure where this sudden barrage of courage is coming from. Like a wave flooding in from the ocean, anger catches me in its current, and I have no ability to turn it back. "Kala ran away from this house last night, and you'll notice I did not call it this home, because it certainly is not that for her."

"What do you mean?" Judith asks, her eyebrows rising in outrage.

"You criticize her constantly. Do you have any idea what you're doing to her self-confidence?"

Judith's indignant huff precedes, "I hardly think I am responsible for the way Kala sees herself. Perhaps if she would keep her hands out of the cookie jar every afternoon, she might like what she sees in the mirror a little more."

My hand itches to smack her judgmental face. I shake my head, words eluding me. I finally manage an incredulous, "Do you not remember what it felt like to be a young girl? Judith, your opinion matters to her."

She shrugs, as if I've stated something ridiculously obvious.

"And that is why I am trying to teach her how a young woman who cares about her looks should eat."

"Is that all that matters to you about Kala? She's your granddaughter. Your son's daughter."

Judith stares at me through narrow eyes, and I wonder, not for the first time, if this is something she questions. When Jeffrey first told her of his intent to marry me, her response had been to ask if I was pregnant. I wasn't at the time, but Kala was born less than a year after we got married, and I think maybe Kala's birth had dashed all her hopes that Jeffrey and I would be short-lived. Sometimes, I wonder if she might have been right to consider it a possibility. Kala had been a surprise, permanently putting to rest any doubts I'd had about the wisdom of marrying Jeffrey.

As if she's read my thoughts, Judith says, "Kala is nothing like my son. Jeffrey had a very disciplined nature."

The words cut like the knife they are intended to be. I could strike back with any number of hurtful reminders of the character qualities that had eventually ruled Jeffrey's choices.

But I stop myself. What good would it do? It is suddenly perfectly clear to me that I no longer belong here. My daughters no longer belong here.

Whatever fear I've been holding onto, worry that I won't be able to make it on my own, awareness that Jeffrey left no will to ensure that his daughters or I would be taken care of should we leave Stone Meadow, all of it rolls away from me like floodwaters bursting free of the dam.

I'm not scared anymore. Not of starting over. Starting over is far less frightening than letting my daughters grow up to be shaped by Judith's constant criticism and bitterness.

Without saying another word, I walk through the foyer and start up the stairs.

"Come back here, Jillian," Judith demands in outrage. "We are not finished."

"Yes," I call back, without turning to look at her. "We are finished, Judith. Permanently."

37

Jillie

KALA IS UPSTAIRS curled into a ball on her bed when I walk into the room. From her doorway, I call her name.

"What?" she mumbles, her head beneath her pillow.

"Pack a suitcase," I say. "We're leaving."

"What?" she asks, bolting up to stare at me with wide eyes. "What do you mean leaving?"

"It's time, honey. Don't you think?"

I know it's what she's wanted, but now that the choice is in front of her, I can see fear of the unknown pulling rank. "Where will we go?"

I don't think I even knew the answer until just now when my daughter so obviously needs to know I haven't lost my mind. "Mr. Callahan has offered me a job. I'm going to take it."

"But where will we live?"

"At Cross Country. In the house where I grew up."

"Really?" Kala asks, a smile of hope breaking across her face.

Seeing it, I have absolutely no doubt that I've made the right decision.

38

Tate

THE BEAGLE DOESN'T leave my side for the next couple of hours.

Since we've both decided he's staying, I make an afternoon appointment with the vet in town to get him checked out. On the drive in, he sits on the passenger seat next to me, looking at the road ahead with keen interest and maybe a little worry.

I reach across and rub his head, thinking the name Audie suits him. I remember reading once that it means old friend, and as he thumps his tail against the seat, I think we'll be that to each other.

Dr. Wendover, the vet, is an older man who retired to the lake area, but decided he missed his patients too much not to go to work every day. I admire his connection to Audie and his obvious appreciation for the fact that I have decided to give him a home.

He gives Audie a full workup, announcing that he's already been neutered and just needs an update on his vaccines. We get the first of those while we're there, and to Audie's visible relief, head for the car.

I make a stop at the grocery store, deciding to risk the store manager's disapproval rather than leave Audie in the car. He trots in next to me with his tail high, as if food shopping is a regular thing for him.

I load up the cart with enough food to stock the refrigerator, debating over the best brand to get Audie. As it turns out, he gets a lot of attention in the store, but no complaints. I roll the groceries out to the car, Audie leading the way.

It's almost four o'clock when we head back down the rutted driveway of Cross Country.

The moment I spot Jillie's car parked at the front of the house, my heart kicks hard, and I wonder if something has happened with Kala. Audie stands in the seat, wagging his tail as we approach, clearly recognizing the vehicle from earlier.

As soon as I pull up beside Jillie's car, I see that she has both daughters with her. I turn the Porsche off and get out, Audie leaping out behind me.

Jillie opens the door and slides out, walking around to meet me, her gaze not quite even with mine.

"Hey," I say.

"Hey," she says back.

"Everything all right?" I ask, glancing at the girls.

She doesn't answer immediately, folding her arms across her chest and looking as if she doesn't know how to get the words out. "That offer you made this morning . . ."

"About turning this place into a horse farm again?"

She nods, still not actually looking at me. "Is that offer still good?"

"It is," I say.

"And the house I grew up in. Could the girls and I stay there for a while?"

"What happened, Jillie?"

"It's time we made another life for ourselves," she says, kicking a sandal against the pea gravel of the driveway. "I don't know why it took me so long to admit it. I just need a little time to figure things out."

"You and the girls can stay in the main house," I say. "I'll take the little house."

"No," she shoots back immediately. "The little house is all we need. I won't have it any other way."

"Jillie—"

"I mean it, Tate. I'm asking enough of you already."

"Would it matter if I told you I don't see it that way?"

"No," she says. "If we can't stay in the little house, I'll have to find somewhere else—"

"You're as stubborn as you always were," I concede, realizing the last thing I want is for her to leave. "The little house it is."

"Thank you. I mean it. And I'll find another place soon."

"It's yours for as long as you want it," I say.

Jillie glances at her car and waves for the girls to come out. They walk over to where we're standing, Kala looking nearly giddy with happiness, Corey reserved and shy.

Audie goes right to Kala, wagging his tail so hard I think he might be in danger of falling over. She drops down onto her knees and gives him a hug, and I can see she's glad he's still here.

Jillie puts a hand on each of their shoulders. "Corey, this is Mr. Callahan. We're going to be staying here for a while."

I drop down in front of her, sticking out my hand and saying, "It sure is a pleasure to meet you, Corey."

She glances up at Jillie, then reluctantly sticks her hand out to shake mine.

"We have a house," she says, glancing back at Jillie again. "Why do we need to stay here?"

"I hear you like horses," I say.

She looks at me suspiciously, and then, "Yeah. Why?"

"I'd like to turn this place into a horse farm again, and your mom's agreed to help me do it."

"Really?" she asks, interested despite an obvious desire not to be.

"I hear you're a good rider too."

"Not as good as Kala."

"I started before you," Kala says, and I admire the way she stands up for Corey.

"I feel sure both of you will be a real help in getting this place back in shape."

Corey's expression has brightened considerably. She slips her hand in Jillie's and says, "That sounds fun."

Jillie pulls her up close and says, "It will be."

Jillie's smile might convince her daughters, but it doesn't fool me. I see her apprehension, her fear that she has done the wrong thing in leaving the Taylor house. I decide then and there to prove her wrong.

39

Jillie

IT DOESN'T TAKE long to bring the few suitcases we brought with us inside the house. Tate insists on helping. I step through the front door first, a little stunned to see that it looks much the same as it had when I'd lived here with my dad years ago.

The sofa has been replaced, but the dining room table is the same, along with the remaining pieces of furniture scattered about. Some of them have been moved, as if someone considered taking them from the house but then changed their mind.

A sob strikes me in the chest, taking me by such surprise that I actually bend into it.

Tate reaches for my arm, turning me to face him. "Are you okay?"

"Yes," I say, feeling suddenly ridiculous. "I . . . it's been a long time."

"Jillie, I'm happy for all of you to stay at the other house."

I shake my head and force a smile. "I think it's just been a long day."

"How about I make dinner for us all?"

"You don't have to do that, Tate," I start to protest.

"I'd like to. And besides, we can start talking up a plan for the place."

"Are you sure?"

"I am. Just don't expect a Michelin Guide rating."

"What does that mean?" Corey asks.

"It means we might be better off ordering pizza, but I'll give it my best shot," Tate says.

Corey giggles, and it's nice to hear the sound.

Tate looks at me. "Six-thirty sound good?"

"Yes," I say. "Can I bring anything?"

"Audie and I have it under control. See you in a couple of hours."

As he lets himself out the door and heads across the yard to the big house, I'm struck with the realization that for the first time in a very long while, I feel happy to be exactly where I am.

40

Angela

WHEN SOMETHING YOU'VE wanted actually happens, and it seems too good to be true, it's hard not to be suspicious.

Angela still can't quite believe they're gone.

Her mother had made the announcement over dinner as if she were relaying some inconsequential gossip about a neighbor they didn't know very well.

"What do you mean they're gone?" Angela had asked, holding her fork in mid-air. "Where did they go?"

"How should I know, Angela?"

"She took the girls with her?"

"Of course, she did," her mother said, with barely restrained irritation.

"This makes no sense, Mother," Angela had said, shaking her head.

"Have you found that Jillian is prone to choices that make sense?"

The words are harsh, even for her mother. "Did you two have an argument?"

"I don't argue, dear."

Angela agrees that she should certainly know that by now. What was there to argue about when your will was never challenged?

She also knows there is far more to the story than her mother is letting on. But whatever had happened, her mother isn't going to be the one to tell her about it.

They finish the remainder of dinner in silence. Angela forces a patience she doesn't feel into the insignificant conversation that makes up the rest of their time at the table.

As soon as she can escape to her room upstairs, Angela flips open the lid to her laptop and Facetimes Poppy.

Impatient, she taps her nails against the desktop until Poppy's smiling face appears on the screen.

"Hey," she says. "I'm getting ready for a date. What's up?"

Of course, Poppy would have a date in the middle of the week. Is there a night of the week when she doesn't? Angela quells her jealousy and says, "Jillian took the girls and left the house today."

"Seriously?" Poppy asks on a note of disbelief.

"She's gone."

"Let me guess. This has something to do with Tate being back in town."

"I heard he bought Cross Country."

"Really?" Poppy asks, incredulous.

"Yeah, amazing, isn't it? That's probably where she's gone." Angela tries to keep her voice neutral, but even she can hear the note of jealousy threatening to surface.

"Now, now, don't forget how much you despise him," Poppy admonishes.

Angela wants to remind Poppy that she's the one who despises him, but that seems like a conversation better left for later.

"Are you worried about Jeffrey?" Poppy asks, chastising.

"How can I not be?" Angela shoots back.

"You could trust me for one thing."

"I do trust you. That's why things have gone as far as they have. I still can't believe Jillie hasn't contested Jeffrey's will."

"What's to contest?" Poppy snaps. "It's what he wanted."

"You and I both know that isn't true," Angela says softly.

Poppy's face turns an unflattering red, visible even with the slight distortion of the computer screen. Her voice is hard when she says, "Do not ever say that out loud again."

For the most part, Poppy presents a carefree exterior to the world. But there have been a few times, and right now is one of them, when Angela realizes there's something completely different beneath the surface. Something a little scary.

"Don't tell me you developed a conscience?" Poppy asks, sarcastic.

"You're the one who resented the fact that she was going to end up with everything that belongs to your family."

"I know," Angela says, looking away from the computer screen so she doesn't have to meet eyes with Poppy. It's true, after all. How can she deny it? It just seems far uglier now than it had right after Jeffery's death when everything had been so confusing.

"Do you want to end up with nothing?" Poppy asks pointedly. "Or better yet, have it left up to your sister-in-law what happens to your future?"

"No," she says softly.

"Then don't forget, this was your idea."

Angela flinches a little at the words. Had it been her idea? She wants to deny the accusation, but a little voice inside reminds her that Poppy is the orator between the two. Arguing with Poppy is a pointless endeavor.

"What if he left a copy of the will somewhere else? What if someone finds—"

"Will you stop?" Poppy snaps. "A person could really get tired of your constant OCD nit-picking at the scabs of every potential little setback."

Angela sucks in a quick breath at the knife-sharp criticism in Poppy's tone. "I'm sorry," she says, contrite. "You're right. There's no reason to be worried."

"There isn't," Poppy agrees. "Just remember, Angela, that I'm on your side. I always have been. What if I hadn't come to work for TaylorMade Industries? You would have ended up with nothing."

Was it true? The question pops up in uncharacteristic defiance. Of course it was true. Jeffrey hadn't cared about anything or anyone but Jillie and their girls. She owed Poppy everything. Even the mere fact that she and her mother were able to stay in the home she'd grown up in without being kicked out by Jillie.

Suddenly, Angela realizes she owes Poppy an apology. As much as she hates admitting it.

41

Tate

AS AN ADULT, I've found life to be pretty predictable for the most part. Work hard. Set goals. Don't expect anything to be handed to you. Remember that perfection doesn't exist.

But tonight. That I hadn't expected.

There's little furniture in the house, but there is a great, old, farm-style table just off the kitchen. Jillie and her girls sit on one side. I'm sitting on the other. Both Kala and Corey are eating the mac and cheese I'd prepared as if it really is Michelin quality, and I'm pretty proud of the effort.

"What's your secret?" Jillie asks, glancing at the girls with a smile.

"Quadruple cheese," I say. "Cheese fixes everything."

"I'll have to get your recipe."

"Happy to share it," I say.

The wall sconces throw out soft light. I've left a couple

of windows open, and a late spring breeze dances across the room.

"I never imagined that you would like cooking," Jillie says.

"Neither did I," I agree, with a shrug.

"Where did you learn?"

"I spent some time in a little village in France a few years ago. The whole town smelled like you imagine your grandma's kitchen should smell."

"Who taught you to cook?"

"The owner/chef at the small hotel where I stayed. He saw food as art, a way to create. I actually enjoyed learning another way to funnel creativity."

"Well," Jillie says, "the people you cook for are the lucky ones."

"This is yummy," Corey says, licking her fork.

"Thanks. I can teach you girls how to make it."

"Awesome," Corey says. "I could eat this breakfast, lunch, and dinner."

"I guess that's the ultimate compliment," Jillie says.

"I'm sure your mom's a much better cook than I am," I say to the girls.

"She makes a really good peanut butter and jelly sandwich," Corey says with all seriousness.

Kala rolls her eyes and shakes her head.

"The secret's out," Jillie says.

We make small talk for the remainder of dinner. It's after eight when Kala says, "We have homework, Mom."

"I've got the cleanup," I say. "You all better get to that homework."

"Kala, why don't you go ahead with Corey? I'll help with the dishes and be right there."

"You don't need to—"

"I'm happy to," Jillie interrupts. "Can Audie walk them back?"

"Sure," I say.

Kala brightens at the prospect of Audie going with them. Both girls politely thank me for dinner and head out of the house.

Jillie and I gather the dishes from the table, carrying them to the kitchen in a newly awkward silence. She puts the plates in the sink and begins to rinse them one by one. "I don't know how to thank you, Tate. I feel incredibly indebted to you."

"You don't need to thank me," I say, realizing I am not comfortable with Jillie feeling as if she owes me.

She rinses the last plate, adds it to the stack waiting for the dishwasher, then turns to face me. "Actually, I do."

Her gaze holds mine, and I'm suddenly remembering how easily I could get lost in her eyes. "Jillie—"

She raises a hand to stop me, saying quickly, "I don't know how I'll ever be able to pay you back."

"You don't have to."

She looks down at the floor, crosses her arms across her chest. "I should have left Stone Meadow after Jeffrey died. I'm ashamed that it took Kala running away to make me realize I didn't have a choice."

"Hey," I say, reaching out to tip her chin up so that she is facing me.

"You don't have anything to be ashamed of."

"I do, actually. I knew we weren't wanted there, but I was too scared to try to make it on my own."

"What do you mean on your own?"

She bites her lip, looks down at her hands.

"Jillie," I say. "What is it?"

"Jeffrey . . . he didn't leave anything to me. Or the girls."

"There was no will?"

"There was. But everything went to Angela and Mrs. Taylor."

"Why would he do that?"

"I don't know," she says, looking up at me now, tears in her eyes. She wipes the back of her hand across her face, as if she resents letting me see her cry.

"What about insurance?"

"His policy wouldn't pay because—" she hesitates, and then says in a low voice, "he took his own life."

I feel as if someone has slammed a fist into my gut. Whatever I had imagined Jillie's life at Stone Meadow to be like, it wasn't this.

"I don't care whether he left anything to me or not," she says. "But his daughters . . . I will never understand—"

I drop the drying towel in my hand, reaching out to pull her to me.

"Shh," I say, rubbing my hand across her back. "Damn, Jillie. I'm sorry you've been through all this."

"I don't want your pity," she says, her face pressed against my shirt.

"It's not pity that I feel," I say, my hand going still between her shoulder blades.

"I know I must look like such a fool. There were plenty of people around here who thought I married Jeffrey for his money. They probably think I got what I deserved."

"Anyone who knows you at all, knows that wouldn't be true." I hold her against me, neither of us saying anything for a good bit.

I finally pull back and look down at her. "Can I ask you something?"

She nods.

"Why did you marry him, Jillie?" I hear the hurt

underscoring my own question, wish for a moment that I could take it back, but I need to know.

She shakes her head a little. "I was lost, Tate. After you left, I didn't know what to do with myself. And then when Daddy had the heart attack and I was on my own, I didn't know where to begin. Jeffrey was kind to me. I didn't have the courage to walk away from the security he was offering. I was a coward."

"I'm sorry I wasn't here for you."

"If I hadn't doubted you when Angela accused you of—"

"Don't," I say. "Water under the bridge."

"I'm sorry, Tate. If I could go back and do that differently—"

"We'd both do some things differently," I interrupt.

"I wouldn't trade my girls for anything. So I can't regret my choices."

"I know."

"And you've made a great life for yourself."

"Do you think I wouldn't have traded it all for what you and I wanted together?"

The question clearly surprises her. "Don't, Tate. Neither one of us can afford to go there."

"Down Regret Lane?"

She laughs a shaky laugh. "Yeah."

"Jillie, a good attorney could probably get you a different outcome. Your daughters have a right to—"

"I don't want that," she interrupts. "That's exactly what Mrs. Taylor would expect me to do. She never believed I was anything but a gold digger."

"Then she never made the effort to know you."

"You don't know me anymore, Tate."

"Have you changed so much?"

"Sometimes, I think so."

"When I look at you, I see the girl I used to know."

"I wish I could believe that."

"Believe it."

She's quiet for a bit before saying, "Do you think it's too late for me to—"

"No," I say without letting her finish.

"I really want to help you make this farm what it once was."

"Good."

"But you have to promise me something."

"What?"

"That the moment you no longer want to be here, you'll say so. That you won't do this just because you pity me."

"I don't pity you."

She stares up at me, tears welling in her eyes. I reach out and brush them away with my thumb.

"I believe there's such a thing as starting over. Do you?"

"I want to."

"That's all that matters then."

"You make it sound so simple."

"I think maybe it is," I say.

She squeezes my hand, steps back, and says, "I'd better go check on the girls. Thank you, Tate. For everything."

"Good night, Jillie."

"Good night, Tate."

I watch her walk out of the kitchen, listen to her footsteps in the hallway, and I can't deny the feeling that she's not the only one starting over here.

42

Jillie

I WANT TO act as if everything is normal. I had set
the alarm on my phone for my regular wake-up time of
5:45. I'm just getting out of the shower when I hear a knock
at the door. I fumble for the robe I packed at the bottom
of my suitcase and hustle to the front door, opening it to
find a tray with a pot of French press coffee, a cup, cream,
sugar, and a bottle of orange juice with two glasses.

I pick up the folded note, take in the familiar
handwriting.

*Kind of forgot you would need breakfast. Meager, but
something to get you going.*

It is signed Tate, but he's nowhere in sight. The
kindness of the gesture thickens my throat, and I realize
that it's been a very long time since someone else thought
of me and my needs.

Even the thought makes me feel selfish and self-
centered. My life could have been far more difficult than it

has been to date. But even knowing that, I can't deny that it's nice to have such a gesture directed at me.

I pick up the tray and carry it back inside the house, place it on the kitchen counter before pouring myself a cup of the steaming coffee. The smell is delicious. I add a little cream and sugar and take a sip with an appreciative sigh. I pour a glass of juice for each of the girls and take it into their room, calling them awake with a cheerful, "Good morning, sleepy heads. Time for school."

Kala rolls over with a groan and pulls the pillow across her face. "It's not Saturday?"

I smile at the question. It's something she used to ask me when she was younger every day of the school week. "No. But it's Friday. So just one more day."

"Morning, Mommy," Corey says, in her adorable, sleep-tinged voice.

I sit down on the twin bed next to her, rub my hand across her hair, and say, "How did you sleep?"

"Good," she says. "You?"

"I did."

"What's for breakfast?" she mumbles.

"Juice for starters," I say. "Courtesy of Mr. Callahan."

"He said we could call him Tate," Kala says, pulling the pillow from her face.

"Courtesy of Tate," I correct. "We'll stop for a smoothie on the way in to school. You girls get up and get at it."

I leave the room on a chorus of half-hearted protest, retrieve my coffee from the kitchen counter and take it outside to the back porch.

The old glider swing from my childhood is still there. I sit down on it, slide forward and back again, the instant squeak telling me it's in need of some oil.

Several small paddocks are visible from here, the grass inside each has grown nearly to the top of the board fencing, which is in desperate need of a good spray washing and painting. I remember how these fields had once looked, manicured and taken care of in the way of a piece of property dearly loved by its owner. I had loved it like that too, even though I had no claim of ownership.

The fact that Tate now does startles me all over again. And I wonder how this could possibly have happened, what the truth really is behind his purchasing this place.

Is it about memories, wanting to create something of the past in order to find his way to a new future? And what about my reason for coming here?

I can admit the obvious. It was an immediate solution to my realization that I could no longer stay at Stone Meadow. But I know it's more than that.

Where Tate is concerned, it's always been more than the obvious. I don't have all the answers to my own questions, but there is one thing I know for sure.

I want to help make this place beautiful again. I want to be a part of what Tate envisions for it. Where I will go from here, I honestly have no idea.

Maybe, for now, that doesn't matter. Maybe, for now, all that matters is this new beginning, in this place that had once been the center of my world, Smith Mountain Lake, with its namesake mountain visible in the distance.

It's been a very long time since I've felt this hopeful.

43

Tate

I WATCH THEM leave, from the wide, bay window of the living room at the front of the house. I realize I'm a little sad to see them go, and, at the same time, aware that it's anything but healthy to be forming an attachment to Jillie or her daughters.

Whatever this is, we both know it's not permanent, and I'll be far better off in the long run owning that up front.

I down another coffee, give Audie his breakfast. We both head out the back door off the kitchen to the barn. I'm going to do an inventory of what tools, if any, have been left on the farm. From there, I'll figure out what we'll need to start getting things in shape again.

I walk down the pea gravel drive to the right-hand end of the barn and the tool room I remember being there. The door is unlocked. I open it, flip on the light and am relieved to see an old push mower and a weed eater. That's about it, but it's a start.

I grab a couple of empty, red, plastic gas cans, call Audie out of the room, and then head for the car.

I DRIVE OVER TO Hayden's Marina to get some gas for the mower and the weed eater, Audie on the seat beside me, his head sticking out of the window.

We pull up to the tank next to the dock. A pretty, young girl with light-blonde hair and an instant smile stands next to one of the pumps.

"Good morning," she calls out. "May I help you with something today?"

I pull the cans from the back seat, saying, "Wanted to see if I could get these filled up."

"Regular or premium?" she asks.

"Regular, please."

"Doing some mowing?"

I set the cans down beside the pump. "Yeah. I'll probably be back for a few refills."

"That's a lot of mowing. Are you new at the lake? Haven't seen you around before."

"Sort of. I used to live here. I just bought the old Mason place."

"Cross Country?"

I nod.

"Oh, I love that farm," she says, her pretty smile wide and contagious. "It's nice to know someone's going to get it back in shape again."

"It's gotten a little grown up," I say.

"Yeah, but it won't take that much to get it looking nice again. Hope you've got some help."

"Probably need to look into that."

"I'm Kat, by the way."

"Tate."

A door behind us opens, slams shut. I look around to see a man walking toward us.

"You need some help, honey?" he asks, looking at the girl.

"No, I'm good. I'm sorry," she says, looking at me, "I didn't get your name. This is my dad, Sam. Dad, this is—"

"Tate Callahan," I interject, reaching out to shake the other man's hand.

He looks surprised, saying, "You're the writer. You made the bestseller lists a couple of years ago."

"Yeah," I say, glancing down.

"Enjoyed the book," Sam says. "I'm a big reader."

"He's living on Smith Mountain Lake now," the girl says, putting the caps back on the cans and standing up with a smile.

"We could use some more writers in the neighborhood," Sam says. "Have you met Bowie Dare?"

"No, I haven't," I say, recognizing the other writer's name. "Like his work though."

"Me too. He lives here on the lake now. I'll have to get you two together. You'd have a lot to talk about, I'm sure."

"Be great to meet him."

"Have you had breakfast?"

"Actually, I was getting ready to start some weed eating before it gets too hot."

"Come in and let Myrtle fix you a bite first. Kat here's on hiatus from the kitchen. She's one of our two resident, gourmet cooks."

"Gotta go on strike every now and then," she says, "just so you can stay appreciated. Can your dog come in?" She points to Audie, staring at us with his head sticking over the lowered window of the car.

"Sure. Let me take these cans over, and I'll get him."

Sam leads the way inside the café. Audie and I follow, his tail wagging so hard it's nearly a blur. The smell of wonderful home-cooked food hits me, and I realize how hungry I am.

He waves me over to the open counter that looks into the kitchen. Kat has now joined the woman at the grill, who looks over her shoulder and says, "Now don't be telling me, Sam, that you're already back for seconds."

"We wrangled you up a new customer, Myrtle."

"Well, it's about time," she says. "Morning, sir, what can I get you?"

"Scrambled eggs sounds good," I say, glancing at the menu.

"You should have some pancakes with that," Kat advises. "Myrtle is known far and wide for her pancakes."

"Don't know how I can turn down that endorsement," I say. "A couple of pancakes with the eggs would be great."

"We'll make a silver-dollar one for Audie," Kat says.

As if he knows exactly what she's proposed, Audie thumps his tail against my leg. I reach down and rub the top of his head.

"Interest you in a cup of coffee while you wait for your order?" Sam asks, looking at me with a friendly smile.

"Sure," I say.

He pours us both a cup from the pot at the end of the counter. I follow him to a table by the window. He pulls out a chair. I take the one across from him, Audie curling up at the edge of my chair.

"What brings you to Smith Mountain?" Sam asks, taking a sip from his cup.

"I kind of grew up here," I say. "Been away for a long time. I guess maybe it's one of those pilgrimage things."

"Well, Cross Country's one of the prettiest spots on the lake."

"I worked there in high school, when it was a horse farm."

"The Mason family owned it, I believe?"

"That's right."

"I'm glad to know it's going to be taken care of again. Everyone had high hopes for the last owner, but somehow that didn't work out."

"Hope I can do it justice."

"Tell me about your writing," Sam says, crossing his arms. "Cross Country seems like a good place for that."

"It would be," I agree.

"If?"

"I could actually write," I admit reluctantly.

"Slump?"

"You could say that. Just not sure if it's permanent or temporary."

"Must be a common thing with you writers. Bowie was telling me about something similar that happened to him."

"How'd he work through it?"

"From what he said, I think it ended up being a case of it working through him. He said writer's block seems to hit him when he has something in his life he needs to stop and take a look at. That writing was kind of a hiding place. And if he didn't want to work on his own problems, he could open the laptop and work on someone else's."

I absorb the words, recognize the truth behind them and wonder if my writing block was what allowed me to come back to Smith Mountain Lake and work on some things I'd intended to leave as they were, never look at again.

Kat appears at the table with my breakfast just then.

She sets the delicious-smelling food in front of me, then bends down to put a saucer with a small pancake on it in front of Audie. He lifts his head and licks her cheek, then takes the treat from his plate.

"He likes it," she says, a smile of delight on her face.

"Thank you," I say, realizing I'm really glad to have stopped in here today. Making friends isn't something I've put a lot of emphasis on in the past few years, and it's good to know there are people worth making the effort for.

I dig into my own food, understanding why Audie looks so happy.

"Are you married, Tate?" Sam asks.

"No," I say. "You?"

"I am. To the lovely proprietor of this establishment."

I glance at the kitchen where Myrtle is singing and stirring a big, stainless-steel pot on the stove.

Sam laughs. "Myrtle? She'd be boxing my ears by day two."

I smile. "Is your wife here?"

"She had to run some errands in Roanoke this morning. I hope you'll come back and meet her."

"I'd like to."

"Anyone special in your life?"

I start to shake my head, and then I think of Jillie, and just say, "I'm not sure."

"Good enough. If you decide there is, we'd love to have you both over for dinner one night."

"Thanks," I say. "That's really kind."

"All right then," he says, pushing back from the table. "I've got a few errands to run myself. Need to get them done before Gabby gets back. We're planning a picnic on the boat this afternoon."

"If you're over my way, stop by Cross Country," I say.

"Would love to see it," Sam says.

He calls out "See ya later" to Myrtle and Kat in the kitchen and ducks out the door. Watching him go, I think he is right. Whatever it is I need to figure out about my life, now's the time. The rest can wait.

44

Jillie

AFTER I DROP the girls off at school, I decide to go by Stone Meadow and get another load of our stuff. I dread doing so, but it's never going to get any easier, and it's not fair to the girls to have to do without their things.

I knock at the front door, hoping Lucille will be the one to answer. Thankfully, she does, her eyes instantly brimming with tears at the sight of me.

"Oh, Jillie, why have you left us?" Her voice is hoarse with tears.

I reach out and take Lucille's hands in mine, squeezing once and saying, "I'm sorry. I just couldn't stay here any longer." I can see from her expression that she understands, even though she wishes it weren't so.

"Come in," she says. "Come in."

"Is anyone home?" I ask.

"Only me. Let's go into the kitchen, and I will make you a nice cup of coffee."

I follow her through the foyer to the back of the house,

already feeling like a stranger here, as if I no longer belong. But then I never really did, so this isn't a surprise.

Lucille picks up a coffee carafe from the counter, retrieves a cup from the cupboard and brings it to the table.

"I'll only have a cup if you join me," I say.

She looks a little surprised by this. She never sits and joins the family in this kind of thing, but maybe she understands my feelings, now that I'm not part of the family and their rules do not apply to me.

"Okay," she says, getting a cup for herself and returning to sit at the table.

"Where are you and the girls staying?" she asks, her forehead wrinkling with concern.

"With an old friend," I say.

"Mr. Callahan?"

"Yes."

"I hear he bought the Mason place."

"I'm going to be helping him there for a while and living on the farm in the house where I grew up."

Lucille's worried expression softens a bit. "That is good then. It is like goming home, yes?"

"In a way, it is. Nothing is the same, and my dad not being there makes me sad, but it's only for a little while. Until I can—"

"I understand," Lucille says. "You don't need to explain. Are the girls all right?"

"Yes, and you're welcome to visit them anytime. They love you, and I know they will miss you."

Lucille's tears are again instant. "I only wish things could be different."

"Me too. But they aren't."

"It's not fair. You deserve to be here. This is your home, your children's home, even though—"

"It's okay. It's better this way. I never really belonged here. I'm just sorry it's taken me this long to get the courage to move on with my life."

"You have to do what's right for your girls."

"I'm not sure what is right for them though. Kala—"

"Is a beautiful, young girl who should never have anything other than that suggested to her." Lucille's voice is suddenly adamant. "Especially not from her grandmother."

Lucille never says a negative word against her employer. She's loyal like that, and it is simply not in her nature. But her love for Kala trumps here, and I reach across the table to squeeze her hand.

"I wish that I could ask you to go with us, Lucille. But I simply don't have the means."

"And I wish I had the means to leave here without it mattering," Lucille says softly.

"I'll always be grateful for your friendship. Please know that."

Lucille gets up from the table, brushing imaginary crumbs from her apron and saying, "If we don't stop this, I'll never get anything done today."

I stand up and take my coffee cup to the sink, rinsing it out before saying, "I just wanted to get a few more of our things, if that's okay."

"Of course, it's okay," Lucille says, "and I will help you."

We both know that if Mrs. Taylor or Angela had been here, it would not be okay at all.

UPSTAIRS, I FIND some empty boxes at the back of my closet and begin filling them with clothes.

I leave the things that really don't matter to me, finding there are more of those than the ones that do seem to matter. Once we're done in my room, Lucille rounds up a few more boxes for the girls' stuff.

I don't want to leave their toys, so I start there. Stuffed animals they've had since they could barely walk, a worn giraffe with half an ear missing, a purple bunny that Kala had once refused to go to sleep without. I set them on the bed, unable to put them at the bottom of the box. I open a dresser drawer and pull out the baby blankets I had saved. I press them both to my face and breathe in the lingering smell of baby lotion.

Lucille puts a hand on my shoulder and squeezes once. She opens another drawer and begins taking out Corey's riding breeches and shirts. She fills one box, and I fill another.

"What is going on here?"

I jump at the voice, startled by Judith's sudden, shrill question. Turning to face the door, I instinctively step in front of Lucille. "I'm just getting a few of our things," I say.

"Did you let her in the house, Lucille?" Judith asks, barely restraining her incredulity. "Obviously, you did, since you're helping her remove things that do not belong to her."

"Ma'am?" Lucille says meekly. "She's only getting what belongs to her and the girls. I didn't think you would see anything wrong with that."

"To the contrary," Judith says, her face suddenly infused with red heat. "Anything she obtained here was done so through the generosity of my son. Not that you ever showed appreciation for that, Jillian."

The accusation is so unjust that it stabs through me like a newly sharpened knife.

"Mrs. Taylor," Lucille starts.

"I would advise you to stay out of this, Lucille. It is none of your concern. Go back to the kitchen immediately."

The command sends a bolt of anger through me, and I am suddenly furious with myself for involving Lucille in this. "Judith, please do not take this out on Lucille. She was only being kind."

"Knowing full well that I would not approve," Judith says, looking pointedly at the housekeeper.

A heavy silence hangs in the room, and then Lucille looks directly at Judith. "You are completely right about that, ma'am. I did know that you would not approve. But that does not make it right. How can you treat your own family so shamefully?"

"What?"

Judith's outrage falls across the room, smothering in its intensity. "Lucille, I would suggest you do as I say, immediately," she manages in a choked voice.

Lucille stares at her for a very long moment, and then, "No, ma'am. I don't think I can do that. Not any more. You see, Jillie isn't the only one here who has decided enough is enough. I'm afraid that one day you're going to realize you can't treat people the way you do. I quit, Mrs. Taylor. As soon as I get my things, I will leave the house."

"Lucille—" I begin.

"It is fine, Jillie. We both know this is something I should have done long ago."

Lucille leaves the room then. Judith stares at me with such hatred that I almost feel sorry for her.

"You have five minutes to get whatever you're going

to take, and then you are to leave this house. If I ever find you here again, I will call the police without a single hesitation."

The words fall across me, and all I can think is how poisonous they are and that I need to get out of here as fast as I can. I pick up the two boxes that mean the most, reach for the giraffe and purple bunny, putting them on top.

I walk past Judith and out of the bedroom then, not giving her the satisfaction of looking back.

45

Tate

I'M RUNNING THE weed eater along the board fence when I see Jillie turn in off the main road. She lifts a hand from the wheel as she drives by me. I wave back, noticing she's not smiling, and it looks as if she's been crying.

I remind myself that maybe she doesn't want me interfering in whatever is wrong, but that lasts all of thirty seconds, and I'm walking back to the little house.

When I get there, she's still sitting in the car, staring straight ahead, her hands on the steering wheel, the engine running.

I knock softly on the window. She looks up with a start, wipes at her eyes with the back of her hand and turns off the vehicle.

I open the door, and she slides out with an attempt at a normal-sounding, "Hey."

"Hey. Everything okay?"

"Yeah," she says. "I just—"

She doesn't finish the sentence, tears sliding down her cheeks as she shakes her head.

"What happened?" I ask, reaching out to pull her against me.

"I got Lucille fired," she says, the words muffled against my T-shirt.

"Lucille, the Taylor's housekeeper?"

She nods, pulling back a bit but not meeting my eyes. "It's the last thing in the world she deserved. I stopped by the house to get some of our things. No one was there so Lucille helped me pack, and Judith came home and found her helping me."

"She fired her for that?"

Jillie nods.

"That's not your fault."

"It wouldn't have happened if I hadn't been there. I don't understand how she can be so cruel."

"She sounds like a pretty miserable person."

"I feel awful for getting her involved in this mess."

I stare down at her, push a tear-soaked strand of hair back from her face. "I have a feeling it'll all work out," I say.

"She's been with them for twenty years," she disagrees, shaking her head.

"Maybe it's a blessing in disguise."

Jillie wipes her face with both hands. "You must think all I do is cry."

"I don't think that. Why don't we get your mind on something different? Let's go take a look at the barn and see what kind of work we'll need to do to get it back in shape."

She nods once. "Let me go change my clothes."

"Meet you there in twenty minutes?"

"Sure," she says, turning toward the little house.

"Jillie?"

She glances over her shoulders. "Yeah?"

"What's Lucille's last name?

"Nichols," she says. "Lucille Nichols. Why?"

I shrug. "I just thought I might have remembered her."

46

Jillie

I DETERMINE TO figure out some way to help Lucille, but for now I pull myself together and put my focus on this first piece of the farm I might somehow affect in a positive way. If I can start supporting myself and the girls, maybe I'll have something to offer Lucille as well.

I've brought along a notepad and pen, and I start making a list as soon as I walk inside the barn where I had spent my youth.

Memories scatter through my mind, things I've not let myself think about for so long. I see the sweet faces of the horses who used to hang their heads over the stall doors, whinnying for a carrot when they would see me come in. I see my dad rolling a wheelbarrow of hay down the center aisle, throwing each horse a flake of second-cutting, orchard grass. I hear his soft whistling but can't remember the name of the tune.

It makes me both sad and happy to be here. It's like

visiting my old life but knowing it's temporary and that I will once again have to let it go.

"Hey," Tate says, appearing at the main entrance of the barn.

I wave my notepad in his direction, saying, "Ready to make a list?"

"Let's get at it."

We spend the next hour or so walking from one end of the barn to the other, immediately writing down the obvious, talking over the less obvious. The barn is in better shape than I would have expected. All the old bones are there. For the most part, it just needs a thorough spray washing, some stall boards repaired here and there, a few overhead light bulbs replaced, a plumber to check out the stalls' electric water troughs, and a fresh coat of paint on the outside.

"I expected it would need more," Tate says, standing in the center of the concrete aisle.

"The Masons put a lot into building this barn," I say. "I'm glad to see it's held up well. We could do the spray washing ourselves. They have the machines at the hardware store, and they aren't too expensive."

"You wouldn't mind doing that?" he asks.

I shake my head. "I like working outside. It's warm, so it's a good time to do it."

"That shouldn't surprise me, I guess; but somehow, it does."

"I was a tomboy when you knew me," I say, running my hand across a dusty stall rail.

"You were, but—"

"You thought the Taylors would have changed me?"

"Maybe."

I shrug. "Sometimes, I don't have any idea who I am anymore."

"You're still you, Jillie," he says in a soft voice.

I meet Tate's gaze, my heart thunking hard in my chest. "Are you still you?"

He doesn't answer for several long seconds, clearly considering his response. "I'm not sure I know the answer to that. Maybe I'm here to find out."

"I don't know how to thank you, Tate. You didn't have to do this for me, especially with the way things were between us when you left."

"I know I didn't have to."

"Then why did you?"

"Because we have history. I really don't have that with anyone else in my life. Shouldn't that count for something?"

I know he's right, but I feel suddenly ashamed for my own lack of consideration for that history. "I owe you an apology, Tate."

"Jillie—"

"Please. Let me."

He watches me for a moment, silent.

I take that as acquiescence and say, "I was wrong not to believe you. I really would give anything to be able to take that back."

"It was a long time ago, Jillie."

"I was jealous," I say, the words coming out so quickly that I realize I don't want to give myself a chance not to be completely honest.

"You knew I wasn't interested in her."

"She had everything I didn't."

"Except me."

The words are low and imbued with truth, and I only

wish I could explain how I had been so stupid and gullible. "Angela had everything. She was the kind of girl who could—"

"She wasn't the girl I wanted, Jillie."

Deep down, I know this is the truth. What is it about me that could not accept that all those years ago? "Things would have been so different if I had believed you," I say.

"We can't rewrite history," he says, and I'm surprised there's no bitterness in the assertion.

"Can I ask you a question?"

He nods.

"That night we met on the road, you were angry at me about the article. You're not angry now. Why?"

He scuffs the toe of his boot against the cobblestone floor, shoves his hands in the pockets of his jeans, looking down. "I guess I've come to believe that things happen to get us to the next place we need to be. I think I needed to come back. That's what brought me here. And whatever's going to come of it, well, I guess that remains to be seen."

"You're such a grown-up," I say, smiling a little.

He laughs. "No one's ever called me that before."

We stare at each other for several long seconds. "You think this is where we're both supposed to be for now?"

"I do."

And somehow, I know he's right.

47

Jillie

WE WORK AROUND the barn until it's time for me to pick up the girls from school. I'm the last parent to arrive, and Kala's expression is annoyed as she climbs into the back of the car, Corey's nothing more than happiness to see me. I try to focus on that and ignore Kala's disapproval, but as always, it's the thing that's not right that pricks at me.

"How was your day?" I direct to them both.

"Great," Corey chimes out.

"Okay," Kala mumbles.

"How was yours?" Corey asks, popping her seat belt into place.

"Good," I say, deciding not to tell them about Lucille right now.

"What did you do?" Kala asks, sounding curious despite her posture of indifference.

"Tate and I worked on a to-do list for the barn."

"Is there a lot?" Corey asks, fiddling with the air conditioner vents.

"Nothing we can't handle."

"It's weird that we're not going back to our real home," Kala throws out in complete contradiction to how much she had wanted to leave there only a couple of days ago.

"I like it at Tate's," Corey says. "And besides, you're the one who didn't like Grandma always fussing at you. Now you don't have to worry about that."

I know Corey means well, but a glance in the rearview mirror shows me that Kala's hurt over Judith's constant criticism is still fresh and at the surface. She shrugs and says, "Lucky me."

"Will we be able to bring our ponies to Tate's barn?" Corey asks.

I really haven't let myself think about this until now. I want to give them an honest answer, and the truth is I don't think Judith will agree to letting the girls take them to Cross Country. "We'll have to wait and see. Grandma's not very happy with me right now, so it probably isn't a good time to ask."

"Why is she so mean to us?" Kala barks the question, but I hear the infusion of hurt in the words.

"Honey," I say, meeting eyes with her in the mirror, "I wish had a simple answer for that. I think we just have to go on from here. Maybe one day, she'll realize what she is missing out on."

"And maybe by then," Kala says, "it'll be too late."

48

Kala

SHE KNOWS IT'S not really their home, but despite the barb she had just thrown at her mom, Kala feels a deep sense of relief when the car stops in the driveway at Cross Country.

There's something about the place that she finds comforting, peaceful, unlike the house where she grew up. There, for as long as she could remember, she'd always had this sense of not really belonging. Of not being what was expected, no matter how hard she tried.

The front door of the main house opens, and Tate steps outside. He waves at them and says, "Can y'all come in for a minute?"

"The girls should really get started on their homework," her mom calls back.

"Just for a minute," he says, and Kala notices what a nice smile he has, along with the fact that her mom is walking toward the front door. She and Corey follow, and as soon as they step inside the foyer, Kala notices a familiar smell coming from the kitchen.

"This way," Tate says, and the three of them follow him down the long hallway. He steps aside as they enter the room, and there's Lucille pulling a tray of cookies from the oven.

"Lucille!" Kala cries, running to throw her arms around the woman's aproned waist. Corey follows, and they both engulf the housekeeper they have loved their entire lives in a tight hug.

"Lucille," Kala's mom repeats. "What are you—"

"Lucille is going to help out around here," Tate says.

"He asked, and I accepted," Lucille explains.

Kala looks at her mom, sees the tears rise in her eyes and slide down her cheeks. She has no idea what happened today while they were at school, but she is so happy to see Lucille that she starts to cry too.

"Now, now," Lucille says, patting her back. "We've got a whole tray of cookies to eat before dinner. I think between the five of us, we should be able to get the job done."

"With milk," Tate says, pulling a carton from the refrigerator.

"Last one to get a cookie off that sheet is a rotten egg," Lucille says.

And not a single one of them could be declared the loser.

49

Tate

I'M SITTING ON the front porch just after dark when I hear the door of the small house open. Through the dim light, I can make out Jillie's figure walking up the pea gravel drive.

She spots me as she approaches the steps. "Hey."

"Hey. Girls asleep?"

"Not yet. They're watching a movie on Kala's computer."

"Have a seat," I say, waving a hand at one of the deep-seat rockers.

She stays where she is though, on the other side of the porch rail. "How am I ever going to pay you back for what you've done?"

"I don't want pay back."

"Why did you hire Lucille?"

"It just seemed like an easy way to right a wrong."

"But it was my wrong to right."

"Does it matter who rights it, as long as it gets—"

"Don't say righted," she says, laughing a little.

"Okay, I won't," I say.

She walks onto the porch, takes the rocker beside me. "I'm creating a debt with you I'm never going to be able to repay," she says.

"No debt."

"Big debt."

"Lucille will be a huge help around here."

"I don't deserve what you're doing for me, Tate."

"You don't need to deserve it."

"I think I do."

I don't say anything for several long seconds. When I do, my voice holds a note of vulnerability I wish I could do a better job of concealing. "It's nice to make a little bit of difference in someone's life."

"It seems like you've done a lot of that."

I shrug. "Sometimes, I wonder if anything I've done in my career has meant a thing."

"You wrote a bestselling novel."

"Not sure I'm going to be able to repeat that."

"Before that, you were a Navy SEAL. That's pretty darn meaningful."

"I thought it was, when I was going after it."

"And now you don't?"

I look off into the dark. "I saw enough bad stuff to know our country still needs defending. I'm glad I served. But I think a lot of Americans don't realize that the wall between peace and chaos is made up of real men and women who risk their lives to keep it there. And that there's a cost to that."

"Were you ever scared?" she asks softly.

"Yes," I say.

"I can't really picture you scared."

I don't say anything for a good bit, remembering the hell-hot afternoon I'd come within a hair's width of blowing myself up.

"Tell me," Jillie says, reaching out to put her hand on the back of mine.

I've never told anyone else, have never let myself dwell on the memory.

The few times I have, panic attack blocks of concrete instantly dropped onto my chest. But Jillie's hand anchors me, and I find myself letting the words come out. "We were at the end of a mission in this small town in Syria. Nearly everyone there had been killed by the time we got there. Landmines were everywhere. We were headed out when I saw this little girl standing in the doorway of a house that was missing its roof. She had a dog in her arms, and when she saw us, she started to run toward the Humvee. I knew she could step on a mine at any second. I made my buddy stop, and I just ran for her, praying with every step that we wouldn't get blown up."

"Oh, Tate, dear God. Did you get them?"

"Yeah."

"Then how can you say your career hasn't meant anything? You're a hero, Tate."

"No," I say, shaking my head. "That day had a good ending. There were plenty that didn't."

"How do you not constantly think about the things you saw?"

"In places like that, you have to have a switch that you consciously turn on and off. It was a little like living in two different realities, but you couldn't be in them both at the same time."

"Have you tried writing about your time there?"

"I'm not sure I want to look at it that closely again."

"Even if it helped others to see something that needs to change in the world?"

"Maybe I'm not that selfless."

"I think you are."

I stand and walk over to the porch railing, leaning forward and looking out into the night. "You always thought more of me than I deserved, Jillie."

"Except the one time you needed me to see the truth," she says, coming up to stand beside me.

I feel her arm brush mine, and something kicks to life inside my chest. I turn a little, not completely facing her when I say, "Jillie—"

"You deserved my loyalty," she says softly.

"Bygones."

She reaches out to press her hand against my face. "I didn't even know to be afraid for you when you were in the military."

"I wouldn't have wanted you to be," I say, looking down into her eyes.

"Someone needed to."

"You had another life, Jillie."

"I never stopped caring about you."

"And I never stopped caring about you."

We stand there for countless seconds, the admissions hanging in the air between us. I realize how many times I've thought about the fact that I would never kiss her again, and yet, here we are, just the two of us, desire a completely tangible thing.

"Do you want me to?" I ask, rubbing my thumb across her cheek.

"Yes," she says, without a second of hesitation.

I take my time because when you've wanted something

this long and never imagined you'd actually get it, you have no desire to waste a moment of its enjoyment.

The kiss is soft and reflective. We've been here before. And I remember why no one else's kiss has ever affected me this way. This is Jillie. The girl I left behind. The girl I thought had lost her trust in me. I gather her up in my arms now and deepen the kiss until we are both completely beyond any need to pretend we haven't both dreamed about this.

We kiss until I am at a point of losing all ability to hold back my own need for more. I bury my face in her neck, forcing my hands to stay at the small of her back.

"Don't stop," she says, in a voice filled with the kind of need that makes me want to pick her up right here and now and carry her upstairs to finish what we've started.

But I know it's too soon. And I don't want to mess this up.

"Jillie, you should go."

She pulls back to look up at me with want-dazed eyes. "I don't think I can."

I draw in a deep breath and say, "One more second of you looking at me like that, and every gentlemanly intention I'm holding onto will be right out the window."

She smiles a little at this. "You picked tonight to be a gentleman?"

"Hey," I say, pushing my hand through the back of her hair and leaning down to give her another lingering kiss. "I don't want to be a gentleman. The opposite in fact. But you have two confused little girls waiting for you, and I don't want to add to that."

As if the words push reason back to the forefront, Jillie steps aways from me, smoothing her hands across her hair and adjusting her shirt.

"You're right. I must seem like—"

"The same girl I was never able to get enough of."

"I'm anything but that," she says.

"Through my eyes, you are."

She holds my gaze for a few moments, then steps decisively back, brushing her hair away from her face and saying, "See you tomorrow, Tate."

"'Night, Jillie." Watching her go, I wish I'd asked her to stay.

50

Jillie

I DON'T KNOW why I bothered to go to bed.

Between the tossing and turning and the mortification flowing like lava through my veins, I finally vault off the mattress just before sunrise. The only thing I can think of to dilute my misery is a run.

I pull on a T-shirt, shorts, and running shoes, then peek in at the girls who are still fast asleep. Outside, the late spring air feels wonderful. I decide to stay on the farm, heading for the edge of the largest pasture and running between the tree line and the tall grass in a strip that isn't so grown up.

Twigs from the oak trees to my right break beneath my shoes, the cracking sound the only music to set my pace to. I breathe in a deep gulp of the clean, morning air and feel a bit of my regret from last night start to dissolve.

Maybe I hadn't come across as entirely needy and desperate for a man's touch. Maybe it's only my imagination that has enhanced the details to HD quality.

I trip on a larger stick, catch myself, and slow my pace a bit. What in the world is Tate thinking this morning?

I'm pretty sure I know.

What kind of marriage did Jillie have?

Does she miss her husband so much that any man will do?

As soon as the question throws itself at me, I immediately reject it.

That's not Tate.

Whatever it was that reignited between us last night had nothing to do with Jeffrey. Unfinished is unfinished. And Tate and I are definitely that.

I run to the far end of the first field, hang a ninety-degree left and sprint the first half of the fence-line. When my heart feels as if it's going to beat itself out of my chest, I slow to a walk, dragging in air until my lungs quit screaming.

Unfinished. Unfinished. The word catches tempo with the pulse throbbing in my temples. And then guilt begins to thread its way beneath the rhythm, until it is the only note I hear.

My husband has been dead a year. How can I feel the way I felt last night? What kind of woman am I to act as if I've completely forgotten I'm a widow to a man who took his own life? Our marriage might not have evolved into a fairy-tale definition of perfection, but the last thing I want is for my daughters to think I've forgotten him.

It had taken Tate's pulling away to make me remember this.

I feel my cheeks flush with a heat that has nothing to do with my run.

What would Kala and Corey think if they had seen us kissing on the porch last night?

It would feel like a betrayal to them. I know this without question, and I suddenly feel ashamed of myself for the picture I would have permanently painted in their memories.

The morning air starts to feel cool against the heat of my skin. I pick up my pace a bit and decide that I have to be my daughters' mother before I am anything else. Tate has given me an opportunity to break free from a life I desperately wanted to escape. I want to live up to that opportunity and make a fresh start with my girls. That means putting away any ideas of Tate and me ever being anything other than partners on a temporary journey.

Something in the resolve lightens the weight on my heart. I definitely lost my head last night, and I'm not going to bother making excuses for myself. But starting this morning, today, my being here at Cross Country is going to be about a new life for me and the girls. Moving on. Beginning again.

51

Tate

LUCILLE MAKES THE best cup of coffee I've ever tasted. I'm telling her as much just as the back door off the kitchen opens, and Jillie sticks her head inside.

"Good morning," she says, not quite meeting eyes with me.

"Morning," Lucille says, looking over her shoulder from her spot in front of the stove. "Pancakes were the request for breakfast. You and the girls coming up?"

"Lucille said I could pick anything I liked," I say, noticing Jillie's long legs beneath the running shorts.

"I'm all sweaty," she says, "and the girls are still asleep. Just wanted to see if you were here, Lucille."

"At least have a cup of coffee," I say, holding up my mug. "I've never had better."

"You'll be hard-pressed to beat Lucille's cooking," Jillie says, smiling a little.

"Come and sit down," Lucille scolds Jillie, "before I

start to get a big head." She's already herding Jillie from the door to the table, setting a mug down in front of her.

She takes the chair across from me, but even with the table between us, I feel the zing of current left over from last night. Jillie focuses on Lucille's coffee pouring, but somehow I know she feels it too.

"Thought maybe we could pick up a couple of spray-washers this morning and get started on the fencing," I say. "See what kind of paint is left when we're done."

"That sounds good," she says, taking a small sip from the hot cup.

Lucille places a plate in front of both of us. "Since you're sitting here, you might as well have some of my pancakes. I'll save some for the girls when they get up."

Lucille's cell phone rings. She reaches in her apron pocket and pulls it out, glancing at the screen and saying, "I need to take this. Be right back."

She puts the phone to her ear, says hello, and walks out of the kitchen. That leaves Jillie and me in an instant, awkward cloud of silence. I feel the need to get us back on neutral footing. I set my coffee mug down and say, "Can we please—"

"Not talk about last night?" she finishes for me.

"Seems like we might need to talk about it."

"I'd rather pretend it didn't happen."

"But it did."

"And it won't again."

"That's not what I was hoping for."

"Don't tease me, Tate."

"I'm not teasing you."

She draws in a long breath and says, "We both know that's not a direction that's going to serve either of us—"

I laugh. I can't help it.

She glares at me and says, "What?"

"That's still how you neutralize things you don't want to put importance on."

"What?" she asks again.

"You get all formal and wordy."

"Wordy?"

"It's the reader in you."

She shakes her head a little, as if she can't figure out what to say to me.

"You're incorrigible."

"Another reader word."

At her gasp, I laugh and say, "Okay, I quit. On a serious note, let's not waste energy telling each other last night was a mistake, and it didn't mean anything, and it'll never happen again."

"But that's all true."

"For you, maybe."

"Tate, don't."

We study each other across the table for several long seconds before I say, "I'm not promising anything."

"What do you mean?"

"I'm not promising it won't happen again. Because right now, I really want to come around this table and kiss the living daylights out of you."

She looks surprised by this. And maybe a little pleased. "We have to make a deal."

"What kind of deal?"

"I'm here to help you get this place back to what it once was. Coincidentally, that gives me the opportunity to start a new life for me and my girls. I don't want to mess that up. So if I'm going to stay, last night can't happen again. It's not optional."

"Spoilsport."

"Tate. Seriously."

"I take it this is an ultimatum."

"It is."

"Well, that doesn't leave me much choice, does it?"

"It's a good Saturday for spray washing."

I lean back in my chair, lace my hands behind my head, and give her a long look. I don't bother to hide the fact that I still want her. I know she sees it in my eyes, but she doesn't budge from her stance, so I say what she wants to hear. "I'll be a good boy."

She slides her coffee cup away from her, stands, and says, "All right then. You go get the spray washers, and we'll be ready to get started when you get back. Deal?"

"Deal," I say.

She's out the door before I can add another word. Lucille walks back into the kitchen, saying, "She barely touched her pancakes."

"I don't think she was hungry," I say.

"Oh, is that what it was?" she asks, giving me a look that says she knows better.

52

Kala

IT'S WEIRD WAKING up in a different house. At first, Kala thinks she's back in her grandma's house, and she blinks hard to take in the differences she immediately senses in the room.

There's not much furniture, and what's here isn't nearly as nice as the room she grew up in. But even as she thinks about that, she feels so relieved that she's not at Stone Meadow. This is a small house. That was a big house. There's a feeling of peacefulness here though, and she wouldn't trade it for anything.

She pats the other side of the bed and finds Corey's leg tangled up in the sheets the way she always is in the mornings. She flops and rolls all night. Kala used to find it irritating, but she's secretly glad her sister is in the bed next to her.

The door opens, and her mom sticks her head inside. "Anybody awake?" she calls out.

"Yeah," Kala answers in a groggy voice.

"Lucille's made pancakes, and she's saving some for you."

Kala smiles before she can stop herself. "Really?"

Her mom nods, walks over, and sits down on the side of the bed. She rubs her hand across Kala's hair and says, "How did you sleep?"

"Good." Kala studies her mom's face for a few moments and says, "You look different."

"I just went for a run."

"It's not that. You look happier. Or something."

A flash of what looks like regret registers in her mom's eyes, and Kala feels bad for making the happiness go away. "I just meant maybe things aren't as hard here."

"In some ways, that's going to be true, honey. But I'm going to have to figure out how to make a living. Which means we aren't going to have some of the nice things we're used to."

"Like what?"

"Like maybe not your ponies."

Kala presses her lips together, tears instantly springing to her eyes. The thought of not seeing her precious Munchy stabs her with the same kind of pain she had felt when her daddy died. "That's how Grandma can pay you back for leaving, right?"

"Kala—"

"Don't say it's not true," she says. "I'm not a baby. I can see how things are."

"I'm sorry," her mom says.

"You didn't make her like that. You don't have to defend her."

"She's your grandmother."

"Then she should act like one."

Her mom sighs, looks out the bedroom window where

the sun is now fully splayed across the backyard of the house. "You're right."

There's some little glimmer of satisfaction in hearing the words, but it slips away, and Kala says, "I don't want to be right. I just want us to be happy again."

Her mom leans over and kisses her forehead. "Me, too. Starting today. Tate has a project for us, just as soon as you and Corey finish your pancakes."

Kala likes the light note in her mom's voice. She reaches over to give Corey a big shake and says, "Get up, sleepyhead! We've got stuff to do."

53

Jillie

THE DAY TURNS out to be a hot one. Mid-eighties, which is a bit unusual for May but perfect for the task we've taken on.

Tate arrives back at the house just before ten with the two spray washers. He runs a multitude of water hoses from the pump at the side of the barn and then gets the machines set up at the far end of the biggest pasture, one on the outside of the fence, one on the inside. He and Kala partner up on the inside, Corey and I on the outside. I'm responsible for pushing the machine while Corey sprays the boards. Tate pushes the other machine while Kala sprays.

We're using plain water without bleach. And the idea is that Tate and Kala stay a board's length ahead of Corey and me so we don't end up spraying one another, but that doesn't last for long and within an hour, we're all soaking wet. Audie runs along in front of us, leaping at the arcs of water and barking in what sounds like sheer joy. He's completely drenched as well. It's been a long time since I've heard my girls laugh so much.

Some of the sprayings are accidental, others aren't, but as the fence starts to regain its formerly sparkling white finish, the four of us are getting more direct hits than the fence.

At one point, Lucille steps out of the house and calls across the field, "What on earth is going on out there?"

Kala waves at her and calls out, "Just working, Lucille!"

"Looks more like playing," she disagrees, shaking her head and ducking back into the house.

"Think we're in trouble?" Tate asks, looking at me.

"Lucille is serious about work," I say. "I don't think playing is allowed."

"All right, then, crew, shape up!" Tate says in a scolding voice, just as Corey hits him square in the chest with a blasting spray of water.

54

Tate

LUNCH IS GRILLED cheese and steamed broccoli. Apparently, Lucille's deal with the girls is that for every indulgence she cooks for them – grilled cheese – they agree to eat something extra nutritious: broccoli.

Surprisingly, they don't argue, devouring both with the appetite of kids who've spent the morning working outside. Arguably, the broccoli is the best I've ever tasted, so I understand their willingness. Both girls, between mouthfuls, are talking nonstop, asking about which pasture we'll do next and throwing out the possibility of doing the barn today as well.

"We might have to put that off for another day," Jillie says. "By the time we finish the next fence, I'll be waterlogged."

"Aww," both girls complain in unison.

"Now, listen to your mama, you two, and eat every morsel of that broccoli or no more grilled cheese," Lucille pipes up from the sink where she's rinsing dishes.

It occurs to me that I could feel like an outsider, listening to how comfortable they all are with one another, saying what they think without fear of being criticized. I could, but I don't.

I feel like part of the circle, part of a family. And that's something I can't say I've ever had before.

It feels nice.

Actually, it feels amazing.

55

Poppy

INCREDIBLE THAT A company the size of TaylorMade Industries has only one person working on Saturday. Is there any wonder profits are down?

Poppy is the one person, of course. She would give herself credit for deserving anything she's gotten from this business, but even that is getting old. She stares at the computer screen, the columns of numbers starting to blend together.

She's been at her desk since six-thirty, halfway expecting Angela to show up out of guilt, if nothing else. But then she should know better. When it comes right down to it, Angela is spoiled and lazy. She takes for granted every single, silver spoon she's had access to since birth.

Poppy is the one who works six days a week minimum. More on average since Jeffrey is no longer here.

She doesn't let herself think about him very often, annoyed for a moment that his name has popped into her mind. For a sliver of a second, she remembers what Saturdays at the office used to be like when they were together. The way in which they'd been free to show their feelings, instead of covering them up behind indifferent exteriors.

She does miss the way he had looked at her. As if she were the purpose he had finally found for existing.

Mostly, Poppy refuses to revisit memories she has no use for. And everything related to Jeffrey falls under that category.

But on impulse, she stands and pushes her chair back from her desk.

She walks out of her office and down the short corridor to the corner office that had belonged to Jeffrey. The door is closed. She turns the handle and steps inside, closing it behind her on the off chance that someone might actually show up today.

Everything is the same. That's a little eerie. But then it's not up to her to clear out Jeffrey's office. That's up to his family. His official family.

Angela had said that Jillie offered to come and do it, but Mrs. Taylor wouldn't hear of it. Had there ever been a woman born with such a control complex?

Maybe the question is a little ironic coming from her.

Poppy is aware of her own narcissistic tendencies. But she would have had the office cleared the day after Jeffrey's exit from this world. That was the difference between her and Judith Taylor. Poppy knew how to call a lost cause exactly what it was.

She walks over to the desk, runs her fingers across the computer keyboard, and then sits down in the oversized leather chair.

How many times had they made love in this chair?

She leans her head back and closes her eyes, letting in another memory.

It had been a rainy, winter afternoon. Poppy had left her own office on the pretense of bringing him a file to review. She'd stepped inside the office, locking the door behind her. She can still clearly recall the look of surprise on his face when she'd begun unbuttoning her dress, neck to hem, opening it wide to let him see the only thing she had on beneath was a thong and thigh-high stockings.

That look on his face, the one of utter captivity, of complete inability to resist her—that was the look she missed more than she would have believed possible. The control she'd had over him, the way she could cup her hand to the back of his neck and pull him straight across the line.

How she missed that.

No other man had ever given her that kind of satisfaction. Because, frankly, she'd never wanted a man in the same way. Yes, there had been physical attraction with other men, but beyond that, above that, was the fact that she, Poppy Sullivan, the preacher's daughter, had snagged the heart of the otherwise unattainable Jeffrey Taylor. The Jeffrey Taylor she had secretly wanted since the day she'd been dropped off at Angela's birthday party in her father's rusty, old car. The Jeffrey Taylor who had ended up marrying Jillie Andrews.

Just the thought ignites a burn deep inside her stomach.

What was it about Jillie that made guys like Tate Callahan and Jeffrey Taylor fall all over themselves to have her? As far as Poppy could see, she was a wet dish rag of a woman who didn't have a clue when her husband had it bad for someone else.

And Jeffrey did have it bad for her at one time. For nearly a year, they'd taken every opportunity they could possibly find to get out of their clothes and into each other.

For a moment, anger lights a ravine of pain up the center of her chest.

When she lets herself think about what they could have had together, she can barely stand the thought that it slipped through her fingers.

Stupid idiot, that's what he was.

They could have made it work. His bratty kids would have gotten over it. And besides, kids grow up. Had he thought they were going to need him forever? That his betrayal of his family was something they would never get over?

She'd like to deny it, but she knows that is exactly what he'd thought.

And those damn antidepressants he'd started taking had only made things worse. She'd told him not to take them, that everybody had bouts of being depressed. What they'd needed was a secret getaway to somewhere far away where no one knew them, and they could be alone and be themselves without his guilty conscience getting between them.

Anger snaps Poppy's eyes wide open, and she's staring at the walls of Jeffrey's office, stunningly aware of his absence. It's like a knife stabbing through her heart, and for a moment, just a moment, she almost lets herself cry.

But she doesn't. Her grief is never going to use that outlet. Crying is weak and spineless. No, her grief is actually going to take a road that means something.

She pushes back from the desk, striding out of the office and slamming the door behind her. Back in her own office, she taps the keyboard to her computer and waits for the screen to pop up.

She logs in under the fake name she'd created early on, long before she'd fully realized what she was going to do with it. Once in, she goes to the website of the Cayman Islands bank where she had set up an account in her own name. Brazen, she supposes, but she had convoluted the tracks of the transfers enough that not one of them was ever going to get as far as this last bank.

Even if someone were deliberately looking.

Like that's going to happen, anyway.

The Taylors are so rich and spoiled, where their money is concerned, that it wouldn't occur to them to notice the reason behind the incremental slipping in the company's profits these past few years. And she is the senior accountant, after all.

She fancies herself a kind of puppetmaster these days. And she isn't done yet. Not by a long shot.

56

Tate

FOR THREE WEEKS, we spend every waking minute
working on the farm. When the girls aren't in school, they
are eager to help. I'm amazed at their diligence and tell Jillie
as much one afternoon when we're working inside the
barn, adding a finishing coat of stain to the stall boards.

"You've done an amazing job with them," I say, dipping
my brush into the stain bucket.

Jillie smiles in the direction of her daughters' laughter.
They're working on a corner stall, and it's nice to hear that
it's more like play to them than work.

"Thanks," she says, running her brush along the edge
of a board. "I'm not sure I get any credit."

"Sure you do."

"Maybe despite rather than because of."

"Why do you say that?"

She focuses on her staining for a stretch of silence.
When she answers, she says, "Things were kind of rocky

between Jeffrey and me, once the girls started to get a little older. I know they felt it."

It's the most direct she's been about the cracks in her marriage, and I'm not sure where to go with this. I decide not asking is the best course.

And eventually, she says, "It didn't start out that way. Jeffrey was kind to me after my dad died. I thought I needed safety, and he definitely represented that. But his mother never accepted me, and, over time, that started to erode whatever good there was between us."

None of it is what I expected to hear. "Why didn't you move out of Stone Meadow?"

"Jeffrey wanted to stay there. I should have insisted we move to a house of our own, but he felt strongly about it, and I guess I didn't have the backbone to make it happen."

I put my brush back in the can, stir the stain, and say, without looking at her, "It sounds like you're being a little hard on yourself."

"No. I let years of my life slip by without admitting I was living a lie. I don't think I can be too hard on myself."

"What do you mean living a lie?"

"I knew there was someone else in his life," she says, her voice low so that it does not carry to where the girls are still giggling as they work.

I put down my brush, reach out to touch her shoulder. "Hey. You don't have to tell me any of this."

"I've never talked about it to anyone," she says, still not meeting my gaze. "Too embarrassed, I guess."

"Why would you be embarrassed?"

"For the obvious reasons, when your husband loses interest in you."

"Couldn't that have been about him and nothing to do with you?"

"I don't think it usually goes that way. It takes two to mess up a marriage."

"Did you cheat?" I ask.

"No," she says quickly, looking up at me in surprise.

"Then how did you mess it up?"

She starts to answer, stops, focuses on the staining, and then says softly, "Things weren't right between us. After the girls got a little older, we both started becoming aware of the chinks in our relationship. When the girls were little and required so much care, it was easy not to look at the distance growing between us. Jeffrey started to stay at the office longer, working on weekends. That kind of thing."

"That doesn't necessarily mean he was having an affair."

"There were other things."

"Like?"

She's quiet for a long moment, and then, "He didn't want me anymore."

The words hit me with a combined stab of surprise and jealousy. Surprise that any man could stop wanting Jillie, and jealousy at the reminder that Jeffrey had once shared her bed and her body. Stupid, considering that I now know and adore their kids, but then my feelings for Jillie have never been defined by logic.

"That was certainly his loss," I manage in a neutral voice.

She looks up at me, paintbrush pausing on the wall, "Thank you."

"Surely, you know that," I say, surprised at the look of gratitude on her face.

She stands, dropping the brush on the paint tray,

wiping her hands across her jeans without meeting my gaze.

"Jillie," I say. "Look at me."

She doesn't right away, reluctant for reasons I can't identify. Until she finally lifts her head, and I see the look in her eyes.

"Any man would be a fool not to want you."

"Tate, don't."

I reach out and tip her chin toward me. "Clearly, you need to hear it. I have no idea what was going on in Jeffrey's head, but I'm pretty sure his choices had nothing to do with anything you did wrong."

"But it did," she says on a broken note.

"How?" I ask, dropping my hand from her face.

She shakes her head a little. "I didn't love him the way I should have."

"You made a commitment to him, and he made the same to you."

"Love and cherish, right?"

"People have made successful marriages on far less."

"I didn't intend for it to go the way it did. After you left, Tate—"

She breaks off there, and I find myself asking, "Do you think we would be together if I hadn't left?"

She looks up at me then, and I see the answer in her eyes, clear as anything I've ever been aware of.

"I can't question anything that's happened, Tate. I have my daughters, and I cannot imagine my life without them."

I know she means it, and listening to the sound of their laughter from the far side of the barn, I agree with her. It's impossible to question anything that resulted in the two of them. "They're incredible," I say.

"Thank you," she says, and I can hear that it means a lot to her. "Can I ask you something?"

"Sure."

"Why aren't you married?"

I suspect she knows the real answer, but I don't think either of us is ready to hear it out loud. And so I say what I've been telling myself every time the question comes up. "I guess I didn't turn out to be the marrying type."

"Ah," she says.

"You sound like you don't believe me."

"It's not that."

"What then?"

"I always thought you did. Seem like the marrying type."

"The one I wanted got away," I say, and the thread of the admission I thought I wasn't ready to make begins to unravel.

She goes completely still, snagging my gaze, and asking softly, "Are you saying you never got married because of me?"

I don't answer for a notable string of seconds, and then I decide there's no reason for me to be anything but honest with her. "I'm saying I never met another you."

We look at each other for what feels like a long time. Tears well in her eyes, and I'm compelled to reach out and brush away the single one slipping down her cheek. "I didn't mean to make you cry."

She shakes her head a little, wipes at her eyes and says, "As hard as I find it to believe, you have no idea how good it is to hear that."

I cup my hand to the back of her neck, lean in, and kiss her softly on the mouth. I let it go on for a minute or so, and then, remembering the girls, I pull back. "You need to see yourself the way I've always seen you, Jillie."

"I don't think the girl you remember exists anymore."

"She's standing right in front of me."

"I wish I could believe that."

"Believe it."

A sudden, high-pitched cry of terror brings us both running out of the stall.

"Mama!"

Kala's voice.

We bolt down the aisle, Jillie calling out, "What is it? What's wrong?"

We reach the stall door, and the answer is immediately clear. In the corner, Kala stands pressed against the wall, frozen with fear. At her feet is a coiled snake. Kala's left ankle is swelling, angry and purple.

Realizing the snake is poised to strike again, I grab a shovel sitting near the door.

Knowing there's not a second to waste, I ram the shovel underneath the snake and fling it against the far wall. "Run!" I shout.

Corey bolts into the aisle, and Jillie grabs the still-frozen Kala. She all but drags her to the door and out onto the concrete floor. "Take them outside, Jillie. Now!"

I hear her leaving the barn with the two crying girls. I see the snake in the corner of the stall, about to slip through a hole at the base of the wall. Before I can get to it with the shovel, it disappears.

Outside, I find Kala and Corey huddled together. Jillie is running toward the house.

"Mama went to get the car," Corey says, her teeth chattering with shock. "She says Kala has to go to the hospital."

I try to subdue my own panic long enough to recall what I learned in the military about snake bites and remember that it isn't advisable to suck the venom from the wound without a device made for it.

I drop to my knees next to her and say, "It's going to be all right, Kala. Stretch your leg out, and be as still as you can. I'm going to call the hospital and let them know we're coming. I grab my cell phone from my back pocket and do a quick search for the number. I hit dial and ask for the Emergency Room. I tell the woman who answers what has happened, and that we think the snake was a copperhead. She asks how long before we can get there, and I say twenty minutes at best.

Jillie races down the driveway in her car, slamming to a stop just short of us. I tell her I'll drive, and she can get in the back with Kala. Corey slides in the passenger seat, and I whip the car around and head for the main road.

A glance in the rearview mirror shows me the absolute fear in Jillie's eyes. "Is there anything else I should be doing? A tourniquet?" she asks.

"It's actually not advised. Just keep her still. I let the hospital know we're coming." I hit the main road and floor the accelerator, painfully aware that every minute counts.

I glance back to see Jillie pulling Kala into her arms and whispering soothing reassurances to her.

"It's going to be okay," I say out loud. "Hang on, Kala. The doctors will have some medicine that should fix you right up."

I catch Jillie's terrified gaze in the mirror and realize how long it's been since I've prayed. But I haven't forgotten how, and I do so for the rest of the drive to the hospital.

57

Jillie

I'VE NEVER BEEN so scared.

Kala's face is as white as the sheet a nurse has just tucked in around her. She's holding my hand so tight it's starting to feel numb. I don't care though. If I could transfuse her pain and the poison from the snake into my own body, I would.

Tate is waiting outside with Corey. A team of doctors are working around Kala's ankle. I try to keep her focus on me, telling her to hang on, she's going to feel better very soon.

One of the doctors steps out of the group and moves to Kala's side, looking at me with serious eyes. "We're going to go ahead and start the intravenous antivenin. It's good that you called ahead and were able to get her here so quickly."

I nod in agreement, immediately thankful that Tate had used the hazard lights to basically drive us here the way an ambulance would have, passing cars at every safe opportunity. "The medicine should work?" I ask, hearing the subdued panic in my voice.

"That's our expectation," the doctor says, patting Kala's arm. "And we'll need to be careful about the risk of infection, of course. We're getting the wound cleaned up now."

A nurse appears just then with an IV bag. The doctor steps aside, saying, "Ellen will get it started it for you, Kala. Don't worry. You're going to be okay."

Even though his voice is kind and reassuring, Kala's grip on my hand tightens, and tears slide from her eyes. I lean in and kiss her forehead. "You're all right, sweetie."

Kala nods a little, but she doesn't let go of my hand, and I can't help but think it has been a long time since she needed me or at least showed it. I want to pull her into my arms and hug her as tightly as I can, but the nurse is administering the IV in her left arm, so I do the only other thing I can do for now. I tell her how much I love her.

58

Angela

SHE'S SITTING ON the side terrace, reading a book on her Kindle that she can't seem to get into, when her mother appears in the open French doorway.

"Apparently, Kala is in the ER with a snake bite," she says in a tone she might have used in mentioning the current weather pattern.

"What?" Angela is instantly horrified. Could it be serious? Despite her differences with Jillie, she is fond of the girls in her own way. "Should we go to the hospital?" she asks.

Her mother's response is further neutral. "I assume Jillian is there to take care of her."

Angela cannot hide her surprise. "But don't you think we should go see her?"

"What would be the point? Jillian has removed them from our lives."

"Mother. She's your granddaughter."

"I'm sure she'll be fine," she says on a flinty note, before turning and walking away.

For a moment, Angela stands in stunned disbelief. Even given everything that has happened with Jillie, how can a grandmother not be terrified for a granddaughter going through something like this?

What should she do?

Normally, there would be no question that she would follow her mother's lead. Jillie had rejected them, taken her daughters, Angela's nieces, and moved out.

But recalling the set to her mother's grim-faced declaration that Kala would be fine, Angela suddenly feels repulsed by her lack of caring. She pictures herself twenty years from now, hard and emotionless. Is that who she wants to be?

Does she want to end up in this house with her mother, alone and bitter?

Without answering the question, she walks past her mother and into the house, retrieving her purse and keys from the armoire near the front door and heading for her car.

59

Jillie

KALA HAS BEEN moved to a private room in the hospital.

She's sleeping when Tate appears in the doorway, holding Corey's hand. Corey looks at Kala, pale and still, and bursts into tears. I open my arms, and she runs to me, sobbing into my shoulder, "Is she going to be okay, Mama?"

I hug her hard against me and say against her ear, "Yes, baby. She's just sleeping."

"I saw the snake first. But I couldn't get the words out before it bit Kala."

"It's not your fault, honey. You couldn't have stopped it from happening."

With her head on my shoulder, Corey reaches across and covers Kala's hand with her own. "Did the medicine hurt her?"

"Just a little needle stick, and that was all."

"Did she cry?"

"No. She was very brave."

"I'm not brave like Kala."

"I think you are," I say, rubbing her back.

"So do I," Tate says, walking over to the side of the bed.

"Thank you for watching after her," I say, looking up at him gratefully.

"We watched after each other. Kala doing okay?"

"Yes," I say. "The doctors said it was good that we got her here so fast. Thank you for the NASCAR-level driving."

Tate smiles at this, and, for the first time in hours, I'm smiling too.

A knock sounds at the door. We both look up to find Angela standing at the entrance. She glances at me and then at Tate, surprise registering on her face, as if she hadn't expected to see him.

"I . . . just stopped by to see how Kala is doing."

I'm not sure what to say at first. The thought of Angela being concerned about Kala is completely out of the blue. "She's going to be okay," I say, hearing the slightly defensive note in my voice.

"Oh. Good," she says. "I'm sorry it happened."

She glances at Tate then, dropping her eyes when she says, "Hello, Tate."

"Angela," he says, in a steely voice that I don't recognize.

To call the moment awkward would be a vast understatement. They stare at each other for a string of moments, old anger surfacing in Tate's eyes, something like regret in Angela's.

Kala makes a sound and shifts on the bed. She opens her eyes to take us all in with a groggy, "Mama?"

"Yes, sweetie," I say, standing to give her a kiss on the forehead. "How are you?"

"Sleepy."

"That's the medicine," I say, brushing her hair back from her forehead.

"Aunt Angela?" Kala squints across the room, clearly surprised to see her.

"Yes," she says, stepping farther into the room. "I just wanted to see how you are."

"Thank you," Kala says politely. "How is Munchy doing?"

"He and Cricket are missing you girls."

"We miss them," Corey says, her head on my shoulder.

Angela nods and says, "I knew you must. Do you have somewhere to keep them?"

"We do," Kala says. "We were working on the stalls today when I—" She breaks off there as if she can't bring herself to remember what had happened.

Angela nods, saying, "Let me see what I can do about getting Grandma to agree to send them over."

The words shock me. My initial inclination is to ask her not to get the girls' hopes up because I can't imagine her having any success with Judith, but I stop myself. I can see that Angela is making an effort, and, regardless of our history, I can't bring myself to ignore the olive branch.

"They would really love that."

Angela brings her gaze directly to mine, and, for a second, I see the flare of an old battle between us. Neither of us looks at Tate, but I'm aware of the triangle of tension.

"Well," Angela says, "I hope you're feeling better soon, Kala."

"Thank you, Aunt Angela. And for Munchy too."

"I'll do my best, okay?"

"Okay," Kala says.

Angela turns and walks out of the room. We all absorb a few moments of silence. I see the indecision on Tate's face, but I'm not surprised when he goes after her. I start to call after him to come back, to leave it alone.

I don't really have that right though. His past with Angela is his to deal with.

60

Tate

I CATCH UP with her just outside the front door of the hospital. She's walking quickly to the parking lot, and I follow her until she hits the remote for her car. "We're overdue a conversation, don't you think, Angela?"

She whips around with a startled look on her face, dropping the keys in her right hand. She quickly stoops to pick them up, opening the car door with the obvious intent of slipping inside without answering me.

I reach out and press my hand against the top of the door, preventing her from opening it. "About eighteen years overdue to be exact?"

"I have to go, Tate," she says, unwilling to look me in the eyes.

"Get in the car," I say, taking the keys from her hand.

I walk around to the passenger side, open the door, and slide onto the seat. She hesitates for long enough that I'm thinking she might run. But she gets in, her hands locked on the steering wheel, as if she's prepared to take off even though I have the keys.

"What do you want, Tate?" she asks in a quiet voice.

"The truth. That's all."

"You know the truth."

"Yeah, I do. And you knew it too."

She glances out the side window, but I can see her bite her lip, and a flash of pain crosses her face. She doesn't answer for so long that I'm not sure she heard me, but then she says, "It was a really stupid thing to do."

There is so much regret laced through the response that years of pent-up anger flicker inside me, and I'm suddenly doubting everything that I had thought to be true. I start to ask her what she means, but decide to wait for her to go on.

"You were always nice to me, and you didn't deserve what I did to you."

"That's a hell of a thing to say at this late date. You changed the course of my life. Do you realize that?"

She turns to look at me then, nodding once with a look of shame in her eyes. "I'm sorry, Tate."

"Why are you sorry?" I ask, unable to keep the bitterness from my voice.

"Why not then, when it might have mattered?"

"I wish I had an excuse that would make me something other than what I am."

"And what is that?"

"A puppet, I guess."

It's about as far from an answer I would have expected as I can imagine. "Whose puppet?"

She glances out the window. "I don't blame anyone for what I did except myself. And I don't expect you to forgive me."

"How am I supposed to understand any of what you've just said, Angela? You accused me of trying to rape you."

She looks down at her hands, bites her lower lip. I have a feeling there's something else she wants to say but can't bring herself to.

"Can we please just leave it at the fact that I'm truly sorry, and if I could erase what I did, I would?"

"You think it should be that easy?"

She shakes her head. "I just don't have anything else to offer you."

The rage that had been pounding at my chest twenty minutes ago suddenly loses its fire, and I find myself feeling something very close to pity for Angela Taylor. How many times over the years had I thought about what I would say to her if we ever saw each other again? How I had wanted to cause her the same kind of pain and loss she had caused me. None of those scenarios had ever come close to anything like this.

Before I can give in to the desire to do exactly that, I drop her car keys into her lap, get out, and walk away.

61

Jillie

WHEN AN HOUR has passed and Tate still hasn't come back, I leave Corey with Kala, who is again sleeping, and walk around the hospital to see if I can find him.

I see the back of his head from the side door of the main lobby. He's sitting on a bench in a small park designed to give patients and visitors a respite from the stress of the hospital.

"Hey," I say, walking over to sit down, a couple of feet separating us.

"Kala okay?" he asks, not looking at me.

"She's asleep again."

"That's probably good."

"You okay?"

"Yep."

We're quiet for a few moments, and then I say, "What happened, Tate?"

"Angela apologized," he says, "for falsely accusing me."

"She did?"

He nods, shrugging. "Go figure, huh."

"Why after all this time?"

"No idea."

"Did she say why she did it?"

He shakes his head, then says, "She said something about being a puppet. But then also that she didn't have anyone to blame but herself."

"What does that mean?"

"I don't know. I spent a lot of time thinking about what I would say to her if I ever had the opportunity. Turns out it fell a little flat. I know this sounds crazy, but I almost felt sorry for her."

"The Angela who came into Kala's room earlier isn't the Angela I've known. Even a week ago, I would never have believed she would do what she did today."

"It doesn't change anything that happened, but it was like I was talking to a different person."

I reach across and put my hand on his. He turns his palm up, and it connects with mine. "I wish I had—"

"Don't," he says softly. "It's the past. Let's just leave it there."

I want to protest, tell him again how sorry I am for believing, even for a little while, that he could ever do what Angela had accused him of. But he's asking me to leave it alone, and telling myself it would be selfish not to, I do.

62

Jillie

LUCILLE IS IN the room visiting with Kala when we get back. She looks up with a worried look on her face, saying, "I can't believe this happened."

"I'm okay, Lucille," Kala says, patting her arm.

"Well, I can see that," Lucille says, "but only because you're tough as nails."

The compliment brightens Kala's smile, and she says, "It was a really big snake, Lucille."

"Probably eight feet long," Corey pipes in.

Kala doesn't bother to correct her. "Don't cry, Lucille. I'm fine."

Lucille wipes the back of her hand across one eye, and says, "When you get old, you're allowed to cry whenever you want to. It's one of the few perks."

I walk over and give her a hug, thanking her for coming.

"What can I do to help?" she asks. "I'm assuming Kala will be here overnight."

"Yes," I say. "I haven't really figured out—"

"You stay here with her, and I'll stay the night with Corey."

"Oh, Lucille, would you?"

"Of course, I will. She looks like she's about to fall over. Why don't I take her home, get dinner started, and give her an early bedtime?"

"That would be wonderful."

"I can bring you some dinner back and a change of clothes if you'd like," Tate says, looking at me.

For some ridiculous reason, tears well in my eyes, and I do my best not to brush them away and bring attention to them. I have no reason to cry, except for the fact that it's really nice to have support, real support, from people you care about when you need it.

63

Tate

I DON'T KNOW how Lucille does it, but she manages to get Corey settled and content playing games on her iPad, while fixing a dinner that smells amazing, as well as packing an overnight bag for Jillie.

I eat with Corey, both of us competing for most compliments delivered to Lucille in the course of one meal. Lucille finally tells us to hush and just eat.

She makes a to-go dish for Jillie, and after I run upstairs and take a shower, I head back to the hospital. I've just gotten into town when my phone rings, and I see Lucille's number. I answer, hoping nothing has happened with Corey.

"I just realized I forgot to put Jillie's toothbrush in the bag," she says.

"Okay," I say, relieved that it's nothing alarming. "I'll stop by the drugstore and get her one."

Just inside the Rocky Mount town limits, I turn in at the CVS, run inside, buy the toothbrush and some toothpaste and am getting back in my car when I notice two women in the lot across from me who appear to be having a heated conversation. I realize then that the one in the passenger seat is Angela. And then I recognize Poppy Sullivan. Her expression is angry, and she is speaking quickly, so intent in whatever she's saying to Angela that she doesn't notice me watching them.

It's an odd thing to witness, and I'm still wondering about it when I reach the hospital a few minutes later. Angela and Poppy were friends in high school, but it's a little surprising to see them together now.

I'm pulling out of the parking lot, when Angela glances my way. We meet eyes, and something like guilt flashes across her face before she quickly turns her head and looks the other way.

64

∞

Jillie

THE NEXT FEW weeks feel as if they're made up of pieces of a dream. Things I've hoped for. Once imagined might be part of my life, but long ago accepted as impossible.

Kala's leg continues to heal. She's able to put weight on it again, and the swelling is almost completely gone. A week after getting out of the hospital, she's nearly back to her old self, insisting she can do anything to help around the farm that Corey can.

And it's amazing how quickly the place has come together. Tate hired John Moran, a neighbor down the road, to bring his tractor over and mow the fields. They look immaculate, if empty, of the horses I remember grazing there.

The sixteen-stall barn has a fresh coat of sand-colored paint; the windows and stall doors trimmed in white. I'm in the barn office early this Saturday morning, cleaning the walls and molding, when my cell phone rings. It's not even seven o'clock yet, and I grimace a little at Angela's name on the screen.

"Hey, Angela," I say, hearing the cautious note in my own voice.

"I tried to talk Mother into letting the girls have their ponies. I thought she would eventually agree, but she's having them sent to a sale barn in North Carolina this morning."

"What?" I ask, shock bolting through me. "She wouldn't."

"She is," Angela says, and I can hear the ragged edge of tears beneath the admission. "I don't know why she couldn't just let the girls have them."

It's the closest I've ever heard Angela come to criticizing her mother. "What is the name of the place they're being taken to?" I ask, forcing calm into the question.

"Thatcher's Livestock Sale Barn. It's a two-hour drive."

"Angela, can you please beg her not to? We'll come and get the ponies today. Pay her whatever she wants for them."

"Her mind is made up," Angela says softly, a thread of shame running through the words. "I heard her tell the driver she doesn't want them back, if they don't sell in the regular ring. They'll go to the slaughter ring after that."

A sickening wave of horror and anger floods through me. "Thank you for letting me know."

"I'll text you the address of the place," Angela says.

"Why are you doing this?" I ask her, certain it isn't something she would have once done for me.

"Please let me know when they're safe," she says, without answering my question. She clicks off then, and I stand for a moment, frozen beneath the awful realization that my mother-in-law truly hates me. Worse though, is the fact that she could do this to her own granddaughters out of spite for me.

65

Tate

JILLIE'S VOICE IS nearly frantic when I pick up the phone at just after seven. I listen in disbelief as she tells me about Angela's call. I don't even know what to say in response except that I'm going with them. But the whole time I'm getting dressed, fury burns inside of me, for the heartlessness of Judith Taylor.

Twenty minutes later, we're in the car and heading down Route 40 toward Route 29. I'd made a quick pot of coffee, bringing two cups with us. Jillie pours some from the thermos and hands it to me.

"Where are we going, Mama?" Corey asks in a sleepy voice from the back seat.

"To a horse sale," Jillie answers.

"Are we buying us a horse?" Kala asks.

"Maybe," Jillie says.

"What about our ponies?" Corey asks. "Are we not going to see them again?"

Jillie turns in the seat, and I can see she's trying to

reassure Corey without telling her something that isn't true. "I want you to," she says softly.

Both girls fall quiet then, and Jillie looks out the window, her coffee mug clasped in her hands. I want to tell her everything is going to be okay. But the words stick in my throat, and for the second time in our recent history, I push the speed limit as much as I dare.

66

Jillie

WE ARRIVE AT Thatcher's at just after ten. We'd stopped once for a restroom break, but other than that, drove straight here.

The parking lot consists of two grass fields on either side of the gravel entrance. Trucks with trailers attached fill the rows outside the enormous, metal building. From inside, I can hear the rhythmic voice of an auctioneer.

Tate parks quickly, and we both get out of the car. I ask Kala and Corey to hurry, and they both look at me as if they have no idea why I'm acting this way.

"We don't want to miss out," I say.

Corey takes my hand, and Kala walks next to Tate. At the entrance of the building, we stop at the registration booth. A woman with yellow, blonde hair and heavily penciled, dark eyebrows smiles at us and says, "You folks going in to the sale?"

"Yes," I say. "What do we need to do?"

"I'll need you to fill out this registration form, and that will get you a number for bidding."

"Has it started?" I ask, hastily providing the info requested on the form.

"About an hour ago," she says with a cheerful smile.

My heart drops, and I say a silent prayer that the ponies haven't already been sold. I feel Tate's hand on my shoulder, pushing the fear aside under his soft reassurance.

"If you'd like to preview what's left to be auctioned off, you can take a walk through the barn just to the right of the main building. Here's your number," she says, handing me a paddle board with 340 written on the front. "You're all set."

I thank her, then turn to Tate and say, "Should we walk through first?"

"Let me look inside and make sure they're not already out there," he says close to my ear.

I nod, my heart pounding so hard I can feel it against the wall of my chest. Corey is still gripping my hand, as if she knows something isn't quite right. Kala follows Tate before I can call her back.

Within a couple of minutes, I spot them coming out of the barn. He shakes his head, and we walk quickly to the other barn. Just inside, a man in coveralls and a John Deere cap nods at us and says, "Can I help you?"

"We'd like to see the horses left for sale."

He points at the row of stalls to our right. "Twelve more to go. All these along here."

"Thanks," Tate says, and we glance in the first stall to find a pitiful, old mule staring back at us from a defensive position in the back corner. His hip bones are sticking out, and I can count every rib on his side.

Tate reaches a hand inside the stall to rub the mule's nose, but he doesn't even lift his head, the look in his eyes reflecting the kind of disillusion that leaves a crack in my heart.

In the next stall is a small pony with hooves so long I don't know how he can possibly walk on them. They curl up and over in a curve, and I have to look away because I cannot imagine how painful they must be.

Tate and I exchange a look of disbelief at what we are seeing. We keep walking, this time just glancing in the stalls as we go, neither of us able to linger on the mistreated faces of these animals who have ended up in this place. Kala and Corey walk behind us, and I wish for some way to send all of these poor souls to safety, even as I know that is impossible.

We've reached the last two stalls when Tate stops abruptly and looks at me. The soft whinny coming from the second stall is immediately recognizable. Kala glances at me in disbelief, then runs to the front of the stall, squealing in delight. "Munchy!" she screams.

The pony hangs his head over the door, nuzzling Kala's neck with his soft nose.

And now Corey has found Cricket in the other stall. Tate lifts her so she can reach out and rub the little mare's face.

Both girls look at me at the same time, confusion marring their happy expressions.

"Why are they here?" Kala asks. "I thought Aunt Angela was trying to get Grandma to let us have them."

"She did try," I say quietly.

"But she wouldn't?" Corey asks.

I shake my head.

"Did she send them here?" Kala asks in horror.

I don't know what to say. I am reluctant to complete this picture of their grandmother, but I also cannot lie to my children. "We're here to try to get them back," I say.

"We're buying them?"

"I hope so," I say, praying that I won't have to disappoint them in this.

What if we can't? What if there's some reason why this won't work out? I feel suddenly sick at the thought of having to leave this place without these ponies.

As if he can tell what I'm thinking, Tate puts a hand on my shoulder and says, "Let's go inside and be ready to place our bid."

"Can we stay here with them?" Kala asks, sounding more like a little girl than she has in years.

"Let's all go in," I say, aware now that I have to protect them as much as I can from an outcome other than the one we're hoping for.

We leave the barn, Kala and Corey looking over their shoulders at the ponies until we are in the sale area. Bleacher seats surround a small stage, where a man wearing a vest with "Thatcher Sales" on the front leads in the old mule we'd seen in the first stall of the barn.

Laughter rises up from the seats around us. A smoke-roughened voice to our right throws out, "He don't look like he could pull a fire alarm, much less a wagon!"

I look down at the broken old mule, and something tightens inside my chest, a sob threatening to rise up out of me. I feel Tate's gaze on me, but if I look at him, I'm going to lose it. So I don't.

The auctioneer taps the microphone, and says, "We'll start the bidding at fifty dollars. Who'll give me fifty, give me fifty, give me fifty? Do I hear forty-five, forty-five, forty-five? I've got forty-five in the top right corner. Now give me fifty, give me fifty. I've got fifty. Do I hear fifty-five, fifty five?"

From the corner of my eye, I see Tate raise the paddle.

"I've got fifty-five," the auctioneer says. "Thank you very much. Anybody got sixty?"

"Two hundred," Tate says, raising his paddle again.

I look at him, my eyes wide, but he keeps his gaze on the auctioneer.

"What's Tate doing, Mama?" Corey asks me in a low voice.

"Being a hero," I say and squeeze her hand.

67

Jillie

BY THE TIME it's all said and done, Tate has bought the remaining horses, ponies, and one mule left in the sale. At some point along the way, I stopped feeling as if I should intervene because, to be honest, I don't remember the last time I felt as happy as I feel right now.

The girls' ponies had been the last two to be auctioned off, and as soon as the auctioneer declares Tate the winning bid, I let out a huge sigh of relief, feeling as if a wall of stone has been removed from my shoulders.

"You really did that," I say, turning to look at him now, unable to hide my shock.

His grin is that of a little boy who's just traded for the one baseball card he's been waiting to find. "We had a barn to fill. Think this ought to do it?"

"Did we just go from a hunter-jumper barn to a sanctuary?" I ask, shaking my head a little.

"Is that insane?" he asks.

"No, but it's certainly not going to be profitable."

Just then, both girls launch themselves at Tate, throwing their arms around his neck and hugging him so hard, I think he might fall off the bench behind us.

"Thank you, thank you so much, for getting our ponies back!" Kala squeals.

"How are we going to get all of them home?" Corey asks, pulling back to look at him with a serious face.

"I need to get to work on that," Tate says, standing, as he adds, "your mama deserves a hug too for making all of this happen."

Corey launches herself at me, arms tight around my neck. Kala's hug is less boisterous, but nevertheless, convincing. "Thank you, Mama," they say in unison.

And for the first time, maybe ever, it feels as if my daughters look at me and see something they like and admire. Nothing has ever felt more meaningful.

68

Jillie

FOR THE NEXT FEW DAYS, we work nonstop on the laundry list of things to do to accommodate the fact that we now have twelve out of our eighteen stalls filled.

Tate had hired four different haulers to bring all our new residents home late Saturday afternoon. Tate and the girls and I stood on the porch, watching the trailers roll down the long driveway, one after the other.

Pure joy had coursed through me. All of a sudden, the farm had purpose and meaning. And I was overcome with a heart-deep desire to make something completely wonderful out of Tate's seemingly spur-of-the-moment decision to save each and every one of those precious souls.

We followed the girls, who were running along behind the trailers, cheering and laughing. And then we unloaded the animals one by one, leading them to their individual stalls.

We had managed to round up twenty bales of

excellent, orchard-grass hay from a neighbor down the road. We hung bright red water buckets by each door, filled with cool, clean water. Once we had everyone inside their stalls, and Tate had paid the haulers, we stood, taking turns watching each one munching at their hay, visibly relaxing before our eyes.

I cried watching them. I couldn't help it. I thought of all my aspirations to make it in the equestrian world when I was younger. About the thought of getting back into that world now. And I wonder if any of it could ever be as meaningful as this. I wonder too if Tate had somehow understood this when he looked at the faces of those abandoned and betrayed animals and saw the reward of creating a haven for them. And down the road, maybe others like them.

That first night, Tate and I had stayed up long after the girls fell into their beds exhausted. Making yet another list of items we would need, including hiring someone to help with the stall work.

A full week from the day we brought everyone home, it seems as if they've always been there. Kala and Corey are giving the little pony they've named Zippy a bath in the wash stall. The farrier had come on Monday morning and trimmed her hooves. Her relief had been so evident that I wanted to cry for all the pain she must have suffered for so long.

Her coat had been shaggy and unkempt, most of her winter hair still matted in place, despite the warm weather. I had used clippers to shave all of it off, so that her coat is now smooth and short and so much more comfortable for the summer weather.

Tate has gone into town to pick up some feed at the Southern States store. I'm in the office placing an order for pine sawdust for the stalls when I notice the girls' laughter has gone silent.

As soon as I finish the call, I walk down the barn aisle to see where they are when I hear a familiar voice.

"Where is your mother, dear?"

It's Judith, her dismissive tone raising the hair on the back of my neck.

"I'm right here, Judith," I say, turning the corner to where she's standing at the edge of the wash stall, her arms folded across her chest.

"How can I help you?"

"I'm sure you think you pulled a fast one on me, Jillian. Buying the ponies at auction."

I look at my daughters, their faces frozen with fear, and I know what they're thinking. That she's going to take them back. Over my dead body.

"Girls, put Zippy in her stall. Run back to the house and wait for me there."

"But, Mama," Kala starts.

"Now, please, Kala," I say.

Judith has the decency to wait until the girls are out of the barn before she says, "You do like to have the last word, don't you, Jillian?"

Vitriol underlines each syllable. I say nothing, but simply wait her out.

"The problem is," she says, finally, "so do I." She looks at me, long and hard, before adding, "He was having an affair with Poppy, you know."

The statement slams into me, and I can feel the barbed cruelty of its intent. Amazingly, my voice is neutral when I say, "I knew he was having an affair with someone. And I had told him I wanted a divorce."

Her face blanches, she drops her arms, and I can see

that she hadn't known this. Realization dawns across her face, closely followed by renewed blame for my role in his death. "Well, his suicide must have been quite the convenience for you then."

Throughout the years, Judith has said some harsh things to me, but this one stretches even her boundaries. I feel the blood leave my face, and my fingers throb with the desire to slap the smugness from her expression.

"Did you ever think that maybe some of your harshness might have made life less than bearable for him?"

Her eyes narrow. "That would certainly lessen your guilt, wouldn't it?"

"Actually, no. I have plenty of it regardless."

Surprise flickers in Judith's eyes then, as if this is the last thing she would have imagined me admitting. "If you hadn't been pining after that Callahan boy, your marriage might have had a chance, and my son wouldn't have felt the need to look outside it."

"I only wish that had been true, Ms. Taylor."

The assertion comes from Tate, his voice deep and serious. Judith turns quickly to face him, and I can see that she's thrown by his appearance.

She folds her arms across her chest again and gives him a steely stare. "I suppose you're the knight in shining armor coming to the rescue of those ponies."

"Someone needed to." He stops a few feet back from her, holding her gaze like a magnet. "Just wondering. Did you put any thought into what you were doing to your granddaughters? Or did revenge trump all that?"

"That's none of your business, Mr. Callahan."

"Anything that pertains to Jillie and her children is my business."

Judith throws me an icy glare, I-told-you-so boldly written there. I start to deny her conclusion, but why should I? She'll believe what she wants, regardless of what I say.

"Unless you came here today for some positive reason associated with your granddaughters, I'd like you to leave, Ms. Taylor," Tate says.

Outrage erupts across her face before she looks directly at me. "I came here today to let you know I'm suing you, Jillian, for the stock left to the girls in trust by my son, Jeffrey. I won't have our company being vulnerable to your sudden decision to find some way to access that."

The accusation floors me. It would never have occurred to me to do any such thing. Suddenly, I am dizzy with anger. It erupts from my center like a volcano long dormant, and it is all I can do to keep my voice from trilling upward as I say, "I want you to leave. Now. Do not ever come near my daughters again. You're toxic, Judith. I will not have you poisoning whatever good memories they have of their father. Go. Get out!"

I scream the last two words, and they seem to echo off the ceiling above us.

Judith's face tightens, her lips a thin line, when she says, "You will regret that."

She turns and walks down the aisle, her back straight, her steps measured and even on the concrete.

I turn away from Tate, folding up the water hose and turning off the faucets to give myself something to focus on. It isn't until I hear the engine of her car start that my shoulders fold inward and the pain inside me will no longer be contained. A sob breaks free from my throat, and I feel Tate's arms wrap around me, pulling me against him.

I feel too humiliated to say a word. He kisses the back of my hair, and this soft act of compassion is my undoing. I turn toward him, burying my face against his chest and crying the tears I have denied myself.

We stand this way for a long time, until my sobbing turns to sniffling and then silence.

"It's not your fault, you know," he says, rubbing the back of my hair.

"It feels pretty awful to be this hated."

"Ever think it might be herself she hates?"

I pull back and look up at him with narrowed eyes. "I don't think so."

"She seems like a miserable person to me. Some of the unhappiest people I've known are the ones who try to control everyone around them, only to figure out at some point that it isn't possible."

I consider this, realizing it was the case with Jeffrey. She hadn't wanted him to marry me, had done her subtle and not-so-subtle best to convince him he would be better off without me. But I think it is only today that I truly realize the extent of how deep her hatred went.

I can't quite meet Tate's gaze when I say, "I should have left the marriage years ago."

"Why didn't you?" he asks in a quiet voice.

I pull away from him, start to pick up the sponge and the brushes the girls left in the wash stall. I want to answer the question. But the answer is too humiliating, too painfully illuminating. Because how do I admit that I hadn't thought I deserved the freedom?

69

Angela

SHE'S NEVER SEEN her mother this angry.

She has memories that compete, but fall short by a good measure.

She'd heard the front door slam from her upstairs room. Against her better judgment, she'd walked slowly down the staircase, finding her mother in the living room just off the foyer.

"What is it?" she'd asked.

Her mother whipped away from the window where she'd been staring out at the field beyond, her face transformed by fury. "She's made a fool of this family."

"Who?" Angela asks, knowing full well the answer.

"Your brother diminished the Taylor name when he married her."

"But Jeffrey's gone. And Jillie doesn't live here anymore. You made certain of that."

Her mother's eyes widen in outrage. "Are you questioning my right to want her out of this house?"

"No, Mother," she says, shaking her head. "It's your house. Your right."

Judith folds her arms across her chest, stares at Angela for several long moments. "There was a time when you hated Jillie for owning what you couldn't have."

It's cruel, even for her mother. Angela flinches, lets the words sink in before saying, "That was a long time ago."

"Don't tell me you're not still pining for him. And she still has him. Meanwhile, you're living at home like a nineteenth-century spinster whose dowry wasn't enough to get the man."

Angela's hand flies to her chest, as if she can prevent the dagger edge of the words from penetrating her heart. But she's not successful, and the pain that spreads through her opens her eyes wide to the truth of her relationship with her mother.

"You've always hated me," she says. "Despised the fact that I don't have your backbone. Your willingness to take down anyone in the way of what you want. I tried to be like you. I tried to destroy a life because I couldn't have what I wanted. That's what you would have done, right?"

Judith's hard gaze turns to steel. "Do you think I would have been able to hold this family and the business together all these years if I weren't made of that kind of determination?"

"You mean that kind of ruthlessness?"

A long silence follows the question. "I think it's past time you found a place of your own."

There was a time when the thought would have filled Angela with dread. Making a life for herself without the comfort of the five-star existence she's lived in this home.

But that's not true anymore. Above all, what she wants now is the ability to figure out who she is on her own.

Whether she really is like her mother, determined to put her own needs and desires above all else. Or, if there is more to her than that, it's time she let it have a chance to come to life.

70

Poppy

ANGELA IS NEVER late on Monday mornings. Punctuality is one of her hallmarks. And so, when she wanders in to her office at nine-thirty, looking as if she barely knows she's arrived, Poppy is curious.

Although the coffee at the community pot is a bit stale, she fills a cup and carries it with her to Angela's desk. "Everything all right?" she asks, handing the cup to her and noticing that her hand shakes a little as she takes it.

"Yes, fine," Angela says. "Thanks."

"Crazy weekend?"

"You could say that."

"What happened?" Poppy asks, sitting in the chair across from her.

"I'm going to move out of my mother's house."

Shocked, Poppy manages an even, "Why?"

"Don't you think it's long past due?" she replies with an uncharacteristic snap.

"Does it matter what I think?"

"We both know it does."

"So what was the reason?"

"She's selling the business."

"What?" The word comes out abrupt and instantly rage-tinged, despite her immediate realization that she needs to rein it in.

Surprise narrows Angela's eyes. "It shouldn't be that much of a surprise, should it? I expected her to want to sell it after Jeffrey died. She's never had any confidence in my ability to keep the place afloat."

Poppy forces herself to say the words she knows Angela needs to hear.

"Of course you do. And have. What else has kept the doors open?" It is all she can do not to add any reference to her own contribution. Even though they both know Angela could never have run this place without her.

"Thanks, Poppy," Angela says, looking at her with sincere appreciation.

Poppy thinks how pathetic and needy Angela truly is. No wonder her mother has zero respect for her. Neutralizing her voice, she says, "How soon is she planning to announce the sale of the company?"

"Immediately," Angela says. "She's already talking with investors."

Which means scrutiny of all accounts and records. Poppy has been good at covering her tracks, but the thought of her methods being tested leaves her with an uneasy feeling. "Well," she says, standing from her chair. "It sounds as if we all might be facing some big life changes in the near future."

"I'm sorry," Angela says.

"It's not your fault." Poppy is amazed by her own ability to conceal her real feelings. What she would like to do is scream at Angela for being such a ridiculous pansy where her mother is concerned, for not standing up to her the way anybody with a backbone would. "Any idea when prospective buyers will start coming in?"

Angela shakes her head. "I'll probably be the last to know."

No doubt. Poppy gives her a sympathetic smile. "Maybe the new owners will want to keep you on."

Angela looks surprised by this. "I can't imagine working for anyone else."

I can't imagine them wanting you to, Poppy thinks to herself. "Maybe this is an unexpected opportunity for us both to do something different with our lives."

"You don't seem very upset."

Poppy shrugs. "This might be the excuse I need to finally see what the rest of the world has to offer."

"You mean move away?"

"What's holding me here, other than this job?"

Angela fails to hide her hurt, and it renews Poppy's contempt for her dependent and weak nature.

"Maybe this is a wake-up call for you too," she says.

"Where would I go?"

"Anywhere you want."

"Where would you go?"

Poppy hesitates, as if she has to think for a moment, when she doesn't have to think at all. "I've always wanted to see the Cayman Islands," she says.

"Really?"

"Yeah. Banking is big there. As an accountant, I should be able to get a job, don't you think?"

"I guess so," Angela says softly.

Not that she would need one, Poppy tells herself. Her plan had been to milk the Taylor cash cow for another year or so before striking out on her own, but that will have to change now. She'll need to slow things down a bit, divert Judith's attention long enough to get her plans in place.

"Well," she says, "better get back to work." She leaves the office then, enjoying the feel of Angela's stricken gaze on her the entire way out.

71

Tate

WE NAMED THE mule Elijah. It had been Kala's choice, and it fits him. I've just finished nailing back a board in his stall when I glance out the open top door that faces the field where he is now grazing. He's put on weight quickly, much faster than I would have believed possible, and his previously tattered coat is showing a new gloss.

I credit Jillie with his progress, as well as the others. She came up with individual recipes for them that include things like coconut oil and turmeric that get added to their grain buckets morning and evening. She's spent hours online researching the most up-to-date information on how to get them healthy again. In her tenacity, I had glimpsed the Jillie who once cared for Mrs. Mason's horses, as if they were her own. She'd had a heart for giving them the best she could then, and this group of rescues is no different.

As if he feels my gaze on him, Elijah raises his head from his grazing, spots me in his stall and lets out a long, honking whinny-bray. I can't help smiling every time I hear it. There's something inherently joyful in the sound, and I realize, not for the first time recently, that I'm immensely grateful to be here in this place, doing what we're doing.

It's not as if I'd ever thought to imagine it. Any of it, really. Jillie. Kala and Corey. Lucille. And all these thrown-away souls who seem as grateful to be here as I am.

Zippy, the pony sharing the field with Elijah, trots over and touches noses with the mule. She likes to check in with him every little while, as if she's afraid he might disappear, and she'll be alone again.

I know exactly how she feels. While part of me realizes Jillie has been through a lot and probably needs time to come to terms with it all, another part of me needs to know what all of this means to her. Is it real? Does she want it to last? Am I intentionally tying her to this place with responsibility and commitment so that she can't leave?

I think about my own question for a good bit, forcing honesty into my answer.

Maybe.

72

Jillie

I PULL UP to the barn and start to unload the items I've just picked up at the hardware store in town. I carry a bucket and some supplements inside, setting them down in the aisle, when I spot Tate in Elijah's stall. "Hey," I say.

He turns around, looking surprised, as if he hadn't heard me come in. "Hey. Need some help?"

"Sure."

We walk outside and grab the rest of the stuff from the back of my car, taking it in and setting it next to my first load. "Everything all right?" I ask. "You look . . . unsettled."

He rakes a hand through his hair and starts to shake his head, then says, "Actually, I've been thinking."

"About?" I ask, feeling suddenly uneasy.

"This," he says, waving a hand at the expanse of the barn. "Us. And what we're doing."

"And?"

"I suspect my motives."

"What do you mean?"

He lets out a long breath, and then, "I don't ever want you to think I pressured you into this."

I release my own sigh of relief. "Tate. Do you have any idea what you've done for me?"

Surprise flickers across his face.

"Honestly, I don't know where I would be without you right now. I guess I would still be at Stone Meadow, letting Judith bully my daughter."

"No, you wouldn't."

"You've given us a place to live. And you've given me . . . a purpose I haven't felt in a very long time."

We study each other for several drawn-out seconds, our eyes saying things we're not yet ready to say out loud. He reaches out and touches the back of his hand to my face. "Jillie."

I close my eyes, savoring his touch. And then I feel his arm loop my waist, pull me to him. His kiss is light, testing. I'm the one to deepen it, wrapping my arms around his neck and opening my mouth to his.

Feeling licks through me like a flame finding its way along a line of gasoline. There has never been this with anyone else in my life. I knew it once with Tate and eventually came to accept that I would never know it again.

We are both heated and breathing hard when he takes my hand and pulls me to the center of the aisle where the ladder leads up to the hayloft. "Want to explore some old memories?" he asks with a nearly wicked smile.

I glance at my watch. "I have half an hour before I need to leave to pick up the girls."

"We might even have time to make a new one or two."

I laugh, feeling happy, as I haven't in so long. "When you put it like that," I say and start climbing the ladder.

73

∾

Jillie

AFTER OUR MEMORY-MAKING session in the hayloft, Tate decides to ride with me to get Kala and Corey. We both agree to keep our hands off each other for the duration of the drive, although I'm sorely tempted to pull the car over and pick up where we left off. I'm pretty sure he knows as much because just before we get to the school, he says, "Any chance we can make a few more memories after the girls go to bed tonight?"

Recalling the feel of his mouth on mine, and the way my pulse flutters at the thought, I say, "I sure hope so."

The girls are clamoring into the car then, each of them talking over the other in getting out the highlights of their day. Tate asks them both about the quizzes he'd helped them study for the night before, high-fiving them when they say they'd gotten A's.

We roll down the driveway of Cross Country to the soundtrack of their laughter when Tate tells them how he thinks Elijah proposed to Zippy this afternoon and that he'd caught them rubbing noses again.

"You're silly, Tate," Corey says on a giggle.

"Well, he does cut an imposing figure," Tate says. "I can see why she's so taken with him."

He glances at me, and I see he's teasing me with the double entendre.

"But he's a mule," Kala says. "And she's a pony."

Tate shrugs. "What can I say? When it's right, it's right."

"Was he funny when y'all were young, Mama?" Corey asks.

I smile at her in the rearview mirror. "He had his moments."

"Hey," Tate says. "Sitting right here."

"What's that?" Kala asks, pointing at the mound of boxes in front of the little house.

"I don't know," I say, stopping the car and cutting the engine.

Kala and Corey are out first, running to the boxes. "There's a note," Kala says, waving it in the air. She looks at it, her face instantly crumpling. I walk to her, taking the note when she holds it out to me.

I read the words. "You have no reason to ever set foot at Stone Meadow again. I have made sure that anything that belonged to you or the girls has been returned in these boxes."

Anger bolts up from nowhere, and I have to close my eyes to force back the river of red fury rolling through my veins.

"What is it, Mama?" Corey asks, and in her voice, I hear that she is afraid.

I fold the note and put it in my pocket. "Everything is

okay, honey. Grandma just sent over our things so we can have them here with us."

Kala meets my gaze, and I can see that she wants to call me out on the varnishing of the truth, but she doesn't, clearly wanting to spare Corey the hurt as much as I do.

74

Jillie

TATE INSISTS ON carrying the boxes into the house and storing them in the small room off the kitchen. I let him do so, only after he promises to let me fix him dinner.

Once he's done bringing them in, the four of us head for the barn and get everyone fed. Seeing the animals content and happy, munching away at their hay, diverts my thoughts from Judith's latest slam, and I try to focus on what it means to see the girls happy the way they are here. While the animals eat, they brush each one until they've all been attended to, their coats glossy, their manes neatly combed.

"It's something to see, isn't it?" Tate says when we stand back to take it all in.

"It is. I can't tell you what it means to me to see the girls care so much about them. It makes my heart full."

Tate puts a hand on my shoulder and squeezes softly. "Mine too. That's one of the tricks to life, I think."

"What?"

"The ability to keep refocusing. Turning away from the bad, finding the good again. It's there. And there's always the temptation to let it be overshadowed by what can seem like a never-ending flood of yuck. We just have to keep turning back to the good."

I reach for his hand, lace my fingers through his, and say, "You're part of that good, you know."

"So let's just keep looking back to each other. Deal?"

I nod once, tears in my eyes. "Deal."

75

Poppy

IT TAKES SOME doing, but she is patient when it comes to executing a plan.

When it finally fully lays itself out in her mind, she puts pen to paper and maps out every possible step needed to cover all her bases. She writes down everything she knows about Judith's weekly schedule, based on things she's learned from both Jeffrey and Angela throughout the years. Fortunately for her, she also knows that Judith rarely diverts from her schedule. And that's the case on Wednesday morning when she pulls out of the driveway at Cross Country and heads to town for her weekly book club meeting.

Poppy waits for her to disappear from sight and then drives right up to the house, as she has many times in the past to deliver company papers that need to be signed. She was able to find out through Angela that Judith has yet to hire a new housekeeper. She doesn't expect to draw attention from anyone who happens to be working at the barn as it is a good distance from the main house.

She pulls around back and gets out of the car with a stack of folders in her arms. She knocks repeatedly at the door off the kitchen. There's no answer, so she lets herself in. Once inside, she calls out hello, and when it's clear no one else is in the house, she runs up the stairs to the bedroom at the end of the hall.

The door is open, and she walks quickly through to the bathroom.

She drops the files on the counter and opens drawers until she finds Judith's toothbrush and toothpaste. She picks up the tube, removes the lid and then pulls the syringe from her jacket pocket.

She pops off the cap and inserts the needle inside the toothpaste, slowly pushing the syringe forward so that the liquid antifreeze has time to blend with the paste. It's a very small amount, actually. Not enough to kill her. Just enough to sidetrack her for a bit and maybe make her wish for death.

Once it is empty, Poppy puts the syringe back in her pocket and replaces the lid on the toothpaste. She puts the tube back in the drawer exactly as she had found it, neatly lined up next to the toothbrush.

She catches her reflection in the mirror, staring at the color in her cheeks and recognizing the glimmer of satisfaction in her own eyes. Problem-solving has become a real strength of hers. As solutions go, this one might be her best yet.

76

Angela

IT'S LATE WHEN she arrives at Stone Meadow. She had deliberately stayed at the office long past the time when she'd wanted to leave simply because she had no desire to field off another confrontation with her mother. And so, it's after ten when she lets herself inside the house, walking softly to the kitchen to make herself a sandwich.

The lights are still on, which is surprising, since her mother has a rarely-veered from habit of shutting them all off before she goes upstairs at nine o'clock. Wondering if she has waited up for her, Angela tamps back the surge of dread instantly inspired by the thought.

She drops her purse on a chair and opens the refrigerator when something catches her attention on the other side of the island in the center of the room. The hairs on her arm stand up, as she turns to see her mother lying on the floor in a fetal position.

"Mother!" she screams, running to her. She drops onto

her knees and shakes Judith's shoulder. "What's wrong? Mother! Wake up!"

But she doesn't. Angela takes her wrist to feel for a pulse and finds it barely detectable. She stumbles to her feet and grabs her phone from her purse. She punches in 911 and waits for the operator to answer. "It's my mother," she says. "Please. Send an ambulance."

77

Jillie

ONCE WE'VE COMPLETED the morning routine at the barn, Tate heads to the house to put in a couple of hours of writing. It's the first time he's done so since we moved to the farm, but I don't make a big deal out of it, telling him I'll see him when I get back from picking the girls up at school.

At the little house, I decide to unpack some of the boxes Judith had sent over. The first two contain clothes that still fit Kala and Corey, so I put them away in their individual drawers. There's another with some of their favorite books that I used to read to them. I put those in the keeper pile.

The next box contains some of my winter sweaters. I decide to leave those in storage, because I really don't have room for them here in the small closet.

Sunshine beckons through the window, and I decide to deal with one more box before saving the rest for another day. I pull off the tape and open the lid, surprised to see some of Jeffrey's familiar clothes inside. I can only assume this box was a mistake. Judith would never have knowingly returned any of his things to me.

There's a suit jacket on top. I lift it out, instantly recognizing the faint scent of his cologne. I think how sad it is that he is gone and yet this lingering trace of him still exists.

I can't manage to feel indifference to any of it, even though that would be the most comfortable place to get to. I start to refold the jacket when I feel something in a side pocket. I squeeze the fabric and hear paper crumple. I reach inside and pull out a white envelope.

The logo of our local bank is on the outside. There's something hard inside. The envelope isn't sealed, so I turn it up, and a key falls out.

I stare at it for a moment, wondering what it could be for. I tap the envelope again, and a receipt slides into my hand. The date is the day before he died. The paper acknowledges a visit to a safe-deposit box.

He'd never mentioned having one to me. But then during the last few years of our marriage, that would not have been surprising. Between the time he spent at the office and our mutually increasing desire to avoid acknowledging that our marriage had become a hollow shell, this wasn't likely to have come up.

It's probably nothing.

I put the key back in the envelope and slip it into my pocket.

I DRIVE TO the bank as if on autopilot. As if some part of my brain has made the decision for me. As if I don't have the conscious courage to do it on my own.

I show the bank manager the necessary credentials,

proof that my name is on the account associated with the safe-deposit box. The young woman who helps me makes small talk about the weather, while she leads me to the vault-enclosed wall of boxes. She points out the number to the one I'm looking for and then leaves me alone.

I stand for a minute or more, key in my hand, feeling as if I am about to open Pandora's box. Do I really want to know what's inside? If it's something I will regret learning about, can I close it back up and walk away as if I never learned of it?

Of course not.

I stick the key in, turning it to the right, and the small door swings open.

A single, white envelope occupies the narrow box. I reach for it, notice the name of the law firm Jeffrey had used in the left corner. The back isn't sealed.

Cautiously, I ease the document from the envelope and unfold it. Last Will and Testament. Jeffrey Dentworth Taylor.

I have to reread the words at the top of the page, absorbing each one on its own wave of shock. The date below Jeffrey's name is the day before his death.

My heart starts to pound, and I force my eyes down the rest of the page.

Again, I read through them in disbelief.

Judith had shown me Jeffrey's will, and it had been dated six months before he died, renewed apparently on some whim I had never understood. But this. This. In addition to the trust established for Kala and Corey, the bulk of his stock in TaylorMade Industries had been left to me.

I do not understand how there could be two wills. Would the date of this one invalidate the other?

I close the door to the safe-deposit box and walk quickly through the bank and to my car. Once inside, I call the number at the top of the letterhead, ask the polite receptionist who answers for the attorney I know Jeffrey had dealt with. I give her my name when she asks.

Lawrence Taubman answers with a note of surprise in his voice. "Ms. Taylor," he says. "How can I help you today?"

I draw in a deep breath and respond with, "You can begin by explaining the existence of a will dated the day before my husband died."

He doesn't answer for several seconds, and I can hear him weighing his response. "I'm not sure what you're talking about, Ms. Taylor."

"It's actually Andrews now," I say. "I found a key to a safe-deposit box in which Jeffrey left a copy of a will, expressing very different wishes from the one his mother presented to me a year ago."

"Yes, well, I—"

"Are you aware of this will, Mr. Taubman?"

More silence, and then, "He sent me a text on the day of his death, indicating that he'd written a new will."

"How much did she pay you?" I ask, ignoring the accusation beneath the question.

"I have no idea what you're talking about," he says.

"Judith. How much? It must have been a good bit for you to risk your profession and your reputation."

"Look, Ms. Taylor, Andrews," he corrects. "Bring the document to my office in the morning, and we'll verify it."

"I'm sure you will, Mr. Taubman," I say and hang up.

IT'S ONLY AFTER I get home—why does that word feel so applicable to Cross Country when I have no real claim on the place—that Lucille tells me of Judith's illness.

She's asked me to step into the living room, away from the chatter of the girls who are eating the snack she has prepared them, and tells me in a low voice of the call she had received earlier from Angela. "They don't know what is wrong yet, but she is very sick. She's in the hospital in Roanoke."

"What happened?" I ask, wondering how I can feel such empathy and alarm even after finding out about Jeffrey's will this afternoon and the likelihood that Judith had kept it from me.

"Angela found her last night. She was unconscious on the kitchen floor."

"I'm sorry to hear that," I say. Odd as it may sound, I'm glad to know that I take no pleasure in the news.

"I would like to go see her," Lucille says. "Even after everything that has happened, I spent many years of my life with her."

"You should. You go. When Tate comes down for dinner, I'll let him know where you are."

"Are you sure?"

"Yes," I say. "Go."

She takes my hand and squeezes it once, "I will call you in a bit." She's at the end of the hall, when she turns and says, "If we don't do better than those we accuse, we have no right to complain."

Watching her go, I cannot deny that she is right.

78

Angela

SHE'S SITTING BY her mother's bed, waiting for the next doctor to come in. Lucille has just left, and Angela had almost given in to the temptation to ask her to stay. Lucille had been as much of a loving mother figure as she had ever known, and she misses her constant presence at the house.

In all honesty, she is surprised that Lucille had come at all. It wasn't as if her mother had ever really been kind to her. She remembered then something Lucille had said to her many times over the years. Try to live by your own sense of right and wrong. Not in response to someone else's treatment of you.

She lets the words roll through her mind, staring at this helpless version of her mother on the bed beside her. She's never seen her mother like this. She seems to have aged twenty years in a day. Her skin has taken on an almost gray pallor. Her lips are pale and dry, as if all the moisture has been sucked from her body.

Angela takes her hand between her own, squeezes softly, wishing for a moment that she could infuse some of her own life force into her mother.

Regret swings its inevitable axe, striking dead center in her heart. Why couldn't things have been different between Angela and her mother? Why had there been so much disappointment and unhappiness?

Life is short.

Never had the statement felt so true to her.

A cell phone rings. She recognizes the tone as belonging to her mother's phone and realizes it's coming from the purse she'd grabbed before running out to her car and following the ambulance to the hospital.

She pulls it from the side pocket and sees the name of the consulting firm her mother had hired to evaluate the company in preparation for the sale. She puts the phone to her ear and says hello.

"Judith?"

"Yes," she says, even as she wonders what she is doing.

"We should meet. I've found some discrepancies in reported income and apparent sales. It's large enough to make me suspicious."

"Suspicious?" she asks softly, hoping he won't realize he isn't speaking to her mother.

"Yes. Possibly embezzlement."

"What?" The word comes out sharp and disbelieving. "Who?"

"Someone high up," he says. "And with extensive knowledge of your accounting practices."

"How much?" she asks.

"I'm guessing millions."

Angela feels as if she has been sucker punched. She taps the end call button without saying goodbye. She stares at the screen and then at her mother, still and lifeless.

Clarity hits her in a flash. Millions of dollars taken from the business. There is only one person who could possibly be responsible.

Sickness washes over her in a wave. She grabs her own phone from the nightstand and leaves the room.

79

Jillie

THE GIRLS ARE asleep. Tate and I have said good night over the phone. I grab my purse and keys, then check on them a quick last time. I won't be gone long. I lock the door of the house behind me, slip in the car, and roll quietly down the driveway.

I looked up her address earlier and put it in my GPS. I know the lake area roads by heart, but her house is in one of the newer developments, and I don't want to waste time looking for it.

I question the wisdom of what I'm doing, but there's something I have to know.

I have never confronted the woman I've suspected had an affair with my husband.

It's not that I haven't wondered what that says about me. I have. Many times. But maybe some part of me understood why Jeffrey had looked elsewhere. Admitted that I hadn't loved him the way a wife should love her husband. That maybe I had married him to fill a void in my life. And I've known plenty of guilt for this admission.

Maybe some part of me thought I deserved it.

My daughters, though, are a different story.

They deserve to know why their father chose to leave them.

And I think Poppy has the answer.

THE LIGHTS ARE on in the house when I turn in the driveway. I recognize Angela's car immediately and wonder if I should leave and come back another time.

I lower the window and breathe in the night air. Is this a mistake? There's an argument for leaving the past in the past. Refusing to dig up unnecessary pain.

A sound shatters through the night. A scream follows, and I realize both have come from inside the house.

I get out of the car and run to the front door, knocking once, twice, but there's no answer. I try the handle. It's locked.

I run around the side of the house to the deck at the back, taking the stairs two at a time.

The sliding glass door off the kitchen is unlocked, and I slide it open, stepping in and calling out, "Angela?"

I cross the tile floor, stopping abruptly at the sight of Poppy in the arched doorway. She's holding a gun, pointing it straight at me.

"I heard a scream," I say, finding her gaze and holding it. "No one answered the door."

"It is a little late for a visit, wouldn't you say?" she asks, without lowering the gun.

"Please put that down, Poppy."

"Why don't you join Angela and me in the living room?" She directs me forward with the gun.

I walk past her and down a short hallway to the large, open room where Angela sits on a chair in the middle of the floor, her hands tied behind her back. She meets my gaze with fear in her eyes.

"What are you doing, Poppy?" I ask, trying to force calm into my voice.

"Angela arrived here earlier with some rather unfortunate accusations that I am being left no choice but to deal with."

I look at Angela. "What accusations?"

"Facts," Angela corrects. "Ten million of them."

"I see no reason for you to be so upset, Angela," Poppy says. "It's just money. And you've always had plenty of it. Be honest now. Do you really think I've been adequately compensated for everything I did for your family and TaylorMade Industries?"

"No," Angela says, shaking her head. "I think prison will be adequate compensation for that."

Poppy laughs. "A sense of humor. Pretty rare in you. I like it."

"What are doing, Poppy?" I ask. "This is crazy."

"I might ask you the same. Showing up at my house. Late at night. I could easily think you were a burglar," she says, pointing the gun directly at me.

"Put it down," I say, "before you dig yourself a hole too deep to climb out of."

"Ever practical Jillie. No wonder Jeffrey became so bored with you that he turned to me."

The words achieve their intended effect, and I draw in a deep breath, releasing it slowly. "Was that your interest in him then? To distract him from the fact that you were embezzling from the company?"

"Such an ugly word. I prefer self-compensation."

"Did Jeffrey know?" I repeat.

"Unfortunately, he did. I'm afraid he felt a lot of guilt over his weakness for me. It did turn out to be a rather expensive one."

"You really have no shame, do you?" I say, staring at her in disbelief.

Poppy laughs. "Shame? Such a waste of energy, that emotion. My daddy did his best to drill that particular one in to me. Afraid it never stuck. A girl does what she must."

"And for you that includes using everyone in your life for your own gain," Angela says, bitterness in her voice.

"Any relationship worth its salt should serve a dual purpose," Poppy reasons.

"Was that the purpose of your affair with Jeffrey?" I ask. "To distract him from the fact that you were bleeding the company dry?"

"Have a seat, Jillie," she says, waving the gun at me. "Since we're going to have a heart to heart, you might as well."

When I refuse, she aims the gun at my head and says, "I insist."

"You sent the picture of Tate and me to that rag paper, didn't you?" I say.

"I admit I got a little nosey after a dinner party at your mother-in-law's house," Poppy says. "I wanted to see the room Jeffrey shared with you. Running across that picture of you and Tate seemed too good an opportunity to ignore. I had hoped you two would make up and leave Smith Mountain Lake to live somewhere else, happily ever after, so that you wouldn't be tempted to look into Jeffrey's unfortunate choice of death. In hindsight, maybe it wasn't such a good idea."

My thoughts are racing, running together so that I can

only wonder why I didn't tell someone I was coming here. "Poppy, this needs to stop now."

She smiles, her teeth white and perfectly straight. With her free hand, she tucks a strand of blonde hair behind her ear, saying, "It was his conscience that forced me to make a decision for him."

"What do you mean a decision for him?" Angela asks sharply.

Poppy shrugs. "Sadly, he was going to do a tell-all with Jillie here. And I couldn't let him do that. So I put a little something in his coffee one morning and decorated his desk with the bottles of antidepressants he'd become so fond of."

"You poisoned him?" I manage, my voice breaking.

"It was incredibly easy," she says, and I hear the pride underscoring the words, realizing how much pleasure she gets from thinking she has outsmarted all of us.

"You didn't even ask for an autopsy. And neither did his mother. You must have both thought his life bad enough to justify suicide."

"You're despicable," I say.

"Maybe," she says. "But I'm about to retire a very wealthy woman far, far from here. And actually, you two shouldn't do so badly if Judith ends up succumbing to her ...illness."

Angela looks at me, her eyes going wide in horror. "Did you do something to her?" she asks Poppy, her teeth clenched together in rage.

Poppy smiles. "Nothing you wouldn't have done yourself if you'd had the courage to do so."

Angela bolts up from her chair, screaming, "I'm going to kill you, Poppy!"

She charges at Poppy, the chair making her stumble and then right herself as Poppy points the gun at her.

"I will shoot you, Angela!" she screams.

"Angela, stop!" I yell out, but she keeps charging, and I launch myself toward her just as Poppy aims the gun and pulls the trigger.

I tackle Angela, and we both go down as I hear the awful roar of the gun being fired. Surely, it has missed Angela. And then I feel a sudden, blazing pain in my left shoulder. It's as if that side of my body has been set on fire. I fall away from Angela, collapsing onto the floor.

"That wasn't very smart, Jillie," Poppy says, staring down at her. "But then that particular affliction seems to run in the family."

I gasp, disbelief forcing my gaze to the blood oozing down my arm.

"You shot her!" Angela screams.

"You can blame that on yourself," Poppy says in a calm voice. "Now, what to do? Should I finish you both off? No, that would be entirely too messy and hard to explain."

"Poppy, she's bleeding," Angela says in a frantic voice.

I feel suddenly lightheaded and try to recall anything I know about slowing down blood loss. My thoughts track over one another, and I push away the fog enveloping my brain.

In the pocket of my jacket, I feel the silent vibrating of my phone. I have no idea who could be calling me this late at night, but I slip my hand inside the pocket and slide my finger across the screen, hoping whoever it is will be able to hear.

"Poppy, let us go. You'll never get away with killing us. Your only option is to leave us here and give yourself time to get away. You can tie us up. We won't be going anywhere."

"Jillie," Angela says, sounding shocked, "you're going to die if you don't get to a hospital."

"I don't think Poppy is going to be very accommodating. Your only option is to leave us here in your house—"

"Why are you talking like that?" she asks, suddenly suspicious.

"Poppy. Just go. Take whatever you've gotten away with and give yourself the only chance you've got to get away."

I feel the words sticking against my tongue, and it is all I can do to get them out. A funnel of light starts to swirl at the corner of my vision, closing in around me. The room begins to fade. I reach out, as if I can anchor myself to the present. Please don't pass out. Don't pass out. The last thing I hear is Angela screaming my name.

80

Tate

I STAND WITH my phone in my hand, stunned. Did I really hear what I think I just heard? I can still make out voices over Jillie's phone, but I can't understand what they're saying.

What has Poppy done?

Panic flares up and burns across my chest. I have no idea where she lives, but I grab my keys and run for the car, Googling her name as I go. Then it occurs to me that I should call the police, which I do, praying one of us will get there before it's too late.

I find an address for Poppy under a white-pages listing, just as the 911 operator answers. I give the operator the address and tell her a woman has been shot and then give her what information I had overheard. I realize how completely crazy it all sounds and wonder if she will believe me. But the operator takes the information as calmly as if I have provided her with a pizza order.

Meanwhile, my heart is racing so hard I can feel it beating in my ears.

Keeping the call open while she continues with questions, I slam the car into gear and floor the accelerator, knowing nothing more than that I have to get to Jillie. Please. Please. Don't let it be too late.

I TURN ONTO THE street just announced by my navigation app. I see the house up ahead, the flashing blue lights of police cars and rescue squads angling in from all directions.

I'm a block from the house, when I see a car pull out of the driveway of an empty lot. The car's lights were off but now flick on, and, as I pass, I catch a glimpse of Poppy's face. Should I go after her? What if she has Jillie with her?

I stomp the brake and swing the 911 around in the middle of the street, stripping the gears second to third to fourth until I am right on her bumper. She accelerates the car and swings out of the cul-de-sac onto the main road.

I hit seventy and realize Poppy has no intention of slowing down. The road is narrow, and trees line both sides just past the ditches. Panic roars through me at the thought that Jillie could be in the car, at the very real possibility Poppy might lose control.

I drop back, giving her some space, trying to decide what to do. I slam my palm against the steering wheel, realizing there's only one option. I gear down and floor the accelerator, jerking into the other lane and whipping around her.

If my memory is correct, there's no turnoff for the next couple of miles and a straight stretch somewhere up ahead. I push the speedometer to eighty, then ninety, one hundred, leaving her headlights behind me. Hopefully, she'll just think I'm some impatient jerk who's finally left her alone.

When she's out of sight behind me, I hit the brakes and spin a U in the middle of the road, killing my lights. I wait with my heart thudding, my eyes strained against the black night. I count the seconds, willing my courage to hang on. Fifteen. Sixteen. Twenty-two. Twenty-four.

Just as I reach thirty, the headlights pop over the knoll. I wait another two seconds and then flick my lights back on. She slams the brakes and skids to a stop ten feet from my car.

I leap out and bolt to her door, jerking it open and hauling her out.

She screams and begins clawing at me with her fingernails. "What are you doing?"

One hand on either of her shoulders, I manage through gritted teeth, "Where is Jillie?"

She stares up at me, her face illuminated in the headlights. Her eyes are filled with outrage. "I believe she's dealing with a gunshot wound back at my house," she snaps.

I have never wanted to hit a woman in my life, but it is all I can do now to restrain myself. With one hand at the back of her neck, I reach in and grab her keys from the ignition, then march her across the pavement to the back of the vehicle, clicking the remote to open the trunk.

"You wouldn't!" she screams.

"I would," I say, pushing her backwards into the open space.

She flails the air with both hands. "If Angela had stuck to the story all those years ago, you wouldn't even be here now!"

I go still at the words. "What story is that, Poppy?"

She stares up at me, as if trying to decide whether she's said too much. But the temptation to finish me off proves too great. "You trying to rape her. Although I admit it was a stretch for anyone to believe you would want her."

"So it was your idea then?"

"Angela's never had a good idea in her life," she says on a disdainful laugh.

"If that's true," I say, staring down at her in disgust, "picking you for a friend was the worst one of all."

I slam the trunk shut, pull my car to the side of the road and then slide under the wheel, whipping another U and pushing the limits of the car's engine all the way back to Poppy's house, blanking my mind to anything except Jillie being okay.

81

Jillie

I FEEL AS if I am in a tunnel. I hear the voices calling my name. I hang onto one. Tate. Pleading with me to wake up. Demanding that I wake up. But that's not anger defining my name. It's fear.

I want to assure him that I am coming. But my legs feel as if they weigh a thousand pounds each, my heart stalling against the effort. I try to reach up for him. I can't make my hand move. I'm here in the same room with him. I can see him. Hear him. But invisible walls have begun to close between us, and panic wells up and over me.

"Jillie! Jillie!"

Tears slide down my face, and my eyes slip closed to my name on his lips.

82

Tate

I WAIT BY the side of her bed, her left hand locked between my two.

It's been a full forty-eight hours since Jillie returned to the room from surgery. She has yet to regain consciousness, and the doctors have been unable to give me any idea when that might happen.

They did tell me how lucky Jillie was, that the bullet missed her heart by an inch. When I think of how close I have come to losing her again, it is all I can do to keep breathing around the fear that swamps over me.

I haven't slept. I've tried, but I'm afraid I'll wake up to find her gone, and so it's easier to wait with my eyes open.

Lucille has the girls and has brought them to the hospital several times while trying to keep them on something of a regular schedule. I want to tell them that everything will be all right, that there's nothing to worry about, but I can't make the words come out of my mouth.

What if I'm wrong? What if they are faced with losing their mother when they so recently lost their father?

It's an unbearable question to consider, and so when Jillie opens her eyes sixty-three hours after the surgery, I have never felt such overwhelming relief and gratitude.

Staring into her beautiful face, I know I will be grateful every day for the rest of my life. I take her hand in mine, entwine our fingers and stare into her eyes. "Hi," I say softly.

"Hi," she manages on a whisper.

"It took you a while."

"I dreamed you were here beside me."

"I was. At the regular protest of pretty much every nurse in the hospital."

She smiles a little at this. "The girls?"

"Are fine. Lucille is holding down the fort. They'll be here again this afternoon."

She closes her eyes for a moment, opens them again. "Am I going to be okay?"

"Yes." I lean in and kiss her cheek. "But I won't be until I get an answer from you."

She shakes her head a little and says, "What was the question?"

"Will you marry me, Jillie Andrews?"

She stares at me, clearly surprised. "Have you been waiting for me to wake up so you could ask me that?"

"Counting the seconds and praying I would get the chance to do so. That I hadn't blown it yet again."

"You never blew it. I blew it. I'm sorry for ever letting myself believe you could be anyone other than the boy I knew you to be."

Her voice breaks on the apology, and I move closer to the side of the bed, smoothing my hand across her hair.

"I have absolutely no explanation for the way things go in this world or why people do the things they do. All I know is that there is only one thing that matters from here—our family. You. And those two girls. And the life we've started building together. Nothing matters to me except that. I don't want to let bitterness or regret tarnish any of it. There's only one thing I do want."

"What?" she asks softly.

"To hear you say you'll spend the rest of your life with me."

"Tate." Tears slide down her face. "You don't have to—"

"Yes," I say. "Yes, I do. I have to. I have to know that you'll be mine, and I'll be yours and nothing will ever come between us again."

A smile breaks through her tears, and she nods once, biting her lip. "Then I say yes. I love you, Tate. I've loved you pretty much since the first day I ever saw you."

"And I think you might have been the first person in my life to ever feel that way about me." This time I'm the one with tears in my eyes. "You have no idea what that has meant to me. What it still means to me."

"I guess I better hurry up and get well then. Since we have a wedding to plan, I mean."

"Yes," I say, leaning in to kiss her. "Hurry up."

83

Jillie

One Month Later
IT IS A wedding I never thought to dream of.

Cross Country is the setting, a small gathering of the people we care about waiting at the edge of Smith Mountain Lake to hear our vows. In the field behind us, a group of our sweet rescued ponies and horses stand with their heads over the fencing, taking it all in.

Kala and Corey are our flower girls. It had been their idea that Elijah and Zippy would also walk with them down the grass aisle centered between the rows of chairs on either side.

Both mule and pony make valiant efforts to catch the pink rose petals Kala and Corey are dropping along the way to the front of the gathering where the pastor and Tate await.

I watch them with a smile that beams upward from my heart and wraps me in a warmth that rivals the summer sun high in the sky.

I know I'm not the first person to realize what a winding road life can take. It would be so easy to regret some of the turns mine has taken me on. To wish I had made some different choices.

But on this beautiful, August day that has spared us of Virginia's typical summer humidity, with the backdrop of Smith Mountain Lake before us, I cannot regret a single turn. Because each one has led me here, to this place, surrounded by the people and the animals I love, to this moment, where I am about to pledge the rest of my life to a man I will do my best to deserve.

When the girls and their companions have reached the front, it is my turn. I walk slowly down the aisle to the awareness that everyone in attendance today is truly happy for us.

Lucille sits at the front, her eyes filled with the kind of pride I know my own daddy would have felt on this day.

Angela is sitting next to her, and, as strange as it seems, I know she's happy for us as well. We've all found as much peace with the past as we can at this point, and have chosen not to give it power over our futures. Among us, Poppy is the only one whose choices have resulted in consequences that cannot be untangled. And while some part of me can feel sorry for her, I know that they were her choices.

At the end of the aisle, Tate reaches for my hand, and his gaze is full with his love for me. Part of me knows I have never done anything to deserve this kind of love. But even so, I am grateful for it.

Pastor Owens smiles at us. "Shall we begin?"

We both nod, our hands joined together. We stand quietly as the violinist plays Ave Maria, and I brush the tears from my eyes.

When the last note from the violin fades, Pastor Owens turns to me. "Jillie Andrews. My dear, do you take this man, Tate Callahan, to be your husband? To love and honor, unconditionally, and with your whole heart? Will you care for him, stand beside him, and share with him all of life's difficulties and joys, from this day forward for the rest of your life?"

My response is immediate, my gaze locked with Tate's. I let every ounce of my love for him shine through my two-word answer. "I do."

84

Tate

I WAKE TO moonlight streaming through the window of our bedroom.

Our bedroom.

I roll over in bed to drape my arm across Jillie's waist, pulling her to me, pressing my lips to her neck and kissing her awake.

"Um, you again?" she says with drowsy humor.

"Afraid so," I say, finding her mouth and kissing her further awake, so that she turns to me, her arms finding their way around my neck, our bodies striking up their instant song.

"I'm not sure I'll ever be able to sleep again with you in my bed."

"You'll grow tired of me soon enough," she says, running her hand down the center of my chest.

"Never," I say, lifting her on top of me and providing her with undeniable proof that she is wrong.

A while later, I hold her close in the curve of my arm, my lips against her hair.

"This could be a dream," she says softly, her thumb absently brushing my chest. "It has been a dream. Many times."

"It's not now though."

"No," she says. "It isn't."

"Are you sorry we didn't go somewhere for our honeymoon?"

She shakes her head. "Kala and Corey were ecstatic to be spending the night at Lucille's, and I love the idea of the four of us going somewhere warm when the weather gets cold here."

Outside our open window, a whinny floats up from one of the pastures. "I have to admit I've never been more content with the thought of staying in one place for the rest of my life. I love it here, Jillie. I already love our life together."

"I love it too," she says. She leans up on one elbow, looks into my eyes, moonlight touching the side of her face. "I love you, Tate Callahan."

"Forever will do," I say.

"Forever it is."

About Inglath Cooper

RITA® Award-winning author Inglath Cooper was born in Virginia. She is a graduate of Virginia Tech with a degree in English. She fell in love with books as soon as she learned how to read. "My mom read to us before bed, and I think that's how I started to love stories. It was like a little mini-vacation we looked forward to every night before going to sleep. I think I eventually read most of the books in my elementary school library."

That love for books translated into a natural love for writing and a desire to create stories that other readers could get lost in, just as she had gotten lost in her favorite books. Her stories focus on the dynamics of relationships, those between a man and a woman, mother and daughter, sisters, friends. They most often take place in small Virginia towns very much like the one where she grew up and are peopled with characters who reflect those values and traditions.

"There's something about small-town life that's just part of who I am. I've had the desire to live in other places, wondered what it would be like to be a true Manhattanite, but the thing I know I would miss is the familiarity of faces everywhere I go. There's a lot to be said for going in the grocery store and seeing ten people you know!"

Inglath Cooper is an avid supporter of companion animal rescue and is a volunteer and donor for the Franklin County Humane Society. She and her family have fostered many dogs and cats that have gone on to be adopted by other families. "The rewards are endless. It's an eye-opening moment to realize that what one person throws away can fill another person's life with love and joy."

Follow Inglath on Facebook
at www.facebook.com/inglathcooperbooks

Join her mailing list for news of new releases and giveaways at www.inglathcooper.com

Made in the USA
San Bernardino, CA
29 August 2018